PENGUIN CLASSICS ⓟ DELUXE EDITION

# HEART OF DARKNESS

JOSEPH CONRAD (Józef Teodor Konrad Korzeniowski) was born in December 1857 in Berdyczów (now Berdychiv, Ukraine) of Polish parents. His father, a poet and translator, and his mother were exiled for nationalist activities and died when he was a child. He grew up and was educated informally in Lemberg (now L'viv) and Krakow, which he left in 1874 for Marseilles and a career at sea. After voyages to the French Antilles, he joined the British Merchant Service in 1878, sailing first in British coastal waters and then to the Far East and Australia. In 1886, he became a British subject and received his captaincy certificate. In 1890, he was briefly in the Congo with a Belgian company. After his career at sea ended in 1894, he lived mainly in Kent. He married in 1896 and had two sons.

Conrad began writing, in English, his third language, in 1886. His first novels, *Almayer's Folly* (1895) and *An Outcast of the Islands* (1896), were immediately hailed as the work of a significant new talent. He produced his major fiction from about 1897 to 1911, a period that saw the publication of *The Nigger of the 'Narcissus'* (1897); *Heart of Darkness* (1899); *Lord Jim* (1900); and the political novels *Nostromo* (1904), *The Secret Agent* (1907), and *Under Western Eyes* (1911). His writing, considered "difficult," received considerable critical acclaim, but it was not until 1914 after the appearance of *Chance* that Conrad won a wide public. The dazzling narrative experiments and thematic complexities of Conrad's earlier fiction are largely absent from his later writings, which are pitched to a more popular audience.

Fame saw the offer of honorary degrees and a knighthood—both declined—capped by a triumphal publicity tour in America in 1923. In addition to novels, Conrad produced short stories, essays, and two autobiographical volumes (1906) and *A Personal Record* (1908– the age of sixty-six.

ADAM HOCHSCHILD is the author of *Leopold's Ghost: A Story of Greed,* [...] *ism in Colonial Africa* and *Bury the Chains: P.* [...] *and Rebels in the*

*Fight to Free an Empire's Slaves*. He teaches narrative writing at the Graduate School of Journalism, University of California at Berkeley.

MAYA JASANOFF is the Coolidge Professor of History at Harvard. She is the author of the prize-winning *Edge of Empire: Lives, Culture, and Conquest in the East, 1750–1850* (2005) and *Liberty's Exiles: American Loyalists in the Revolutionary World* (2011), which received the National Book Critics Circle Award for Nonfiction and the George Washington Book Prize, and *The Dawn Watch: Joseph Conrad in a Global World* (2017). A 2013 Guggenheim Fellow, Jasanoff won the 2017 Windham-Campbell Prize for Nonfiction.

TIMOTHY S. HAYES is an instructor of English at Auburn University in Alabama. His research interests include narrative theory and the novel, particularly the works of Robert Louis Stevenson and Joseph Conrad.

# JOSEPH CONRAD

# Heart of Darkness

WITHDRAWN

*Introduction by*
ADAM HOCHSCHILD

*Afterword by*
MAYA JASANOFF

*Notes and Apparatus by*
TIMOTHY S. HAYES

PENGUIN BOOKS

PENGUIN BOOKS
An imprint of Penguin Random House LLC
375 Hudson Street
New York, New York 10014
penguin.com

First published in Great Britain in *Youth: A Narrative; and Two Other Stories*
by William Blackwood & Sons 1902
First published in the United States of America by McClure, Phillips 1903
This edition with an afterword by Maya Jasanoff published in Penguin Books 2017

Introduction copyright © 2012 by Adam Hochschild
Afterword copyright © 2017 by Maya Jasanoff

Originally published in serial form in *Blackwood's Magazine*, 1899.

The filmography, "Telling Africa's Story Today," further reading, character sketches,
and notes by Timothy S. Hayes appeared in the Penguin Enriched eBook Classic
edition of *Heart of Darkness*. Copyright © Timothy S. Hayes, 2008.

LIBRARY OF CONGRESS CATALOGING-IN-PUBLICATION DATA
Names: Conrad, Joseph, 1857–1924, author. | Hochschild, Adam, writer of
introduction. | Jasanoff, Maya, 1974– writer of afterword. | Hayes,
Timothy Scott, contributor.
Title: Heart of darkness / Joseph Conrad ; introduction by Adam Hochschild ;
afterword by Maya Jasanoff ; notes and apparatus by Timothy S. Hayes.
Description: New York : Penguin Books, 2017. | Includes bibliographical
references.
Identifiers: LCCN 2017043105 (print) | LCCN 2017043249 (ebook) | ISBN
9781101613689 (ebook) | ISBN 9780143106586
Subjects: LCSH: Europeans—Africa—Fiction. | Trading posts—Fiction. |
Degeneration—Fiction. | Imperialism—Fiction. | Africa—Fiction. |
Psychological fiction.
Classification: LCC PR6005.O4 (ebook) | LCC PR6005.O4 H4 2017 (print) | DDC
823/.912—dc23
LC record available at https://lccn.loc.gov/2017043105

Printed in the United States of America
17  19  20  18  16

Set in Sabon

# Contents

# Introduction

At the beginning of August 1890, the steamboat *Roi des Belges*—King of the Belgians—a small, boxy, wood-burning stern-wheeler with a funnel and pilothouse on its upper deck, began a four-week journey up the Congo River. At the captain's side was a thirty-two-year-old ship's officer, stocky and black bearded, whose eyes, in some photographs, look as if they were perpetually narrowed against the tropical sun. Konrad Korzeniowski, of Polish descent, had arrived in the Congo some weeks earlier, his nautical experience previously limited to the sea. This was his first trip on the river, and his logbook from the voyage is entirely filled with detailed, businesslike notes about such matters as shoals, sandbars, and refueling points not included on the primitive navigational chart available: "Lulonga Passage. . . . NbyE to NNE. On the Port Side: Snags. Soundings in fathoms: 2,2,2,1,1,2,2,2,2. . . ."

It would be almost a decade before he finally committed to paper a great many other features of the Congo not shown on the map, and by that time, of course, the world would know him as Joseph Conrad:

> Going up that river was like travelling back to the earliest beginnings of the world, when vegetation rioted on the earth and the big trees were kings. An empty stream, a great silence, an impenetrable forest. The air was warm, thick, heavy, sluggish. There was no joy in the brilliance of sunshine. The long stretches of the waterway ran on, deserted, into the gloom of overshadowed distances. On silvery sandbanks hippos and alligators sunned themselves side by side. The broadening waters flowed through a mob of wooded islands; you lost your way on that river as you would in a desert, and butted all day long against shoals, trying to find the channel, till you

thought yourself bewitched and cut off for ever from everything you had known . . .

The European colonization of the African continent, often called the Scramble for Africa, was the greatest land grab in history, and one of the swiftest. In 1870, some 80 percent of Africa south of the Sahara was still under the control of indigenous kings, chiefs, or other rulers. Within thirty-five years, virtually the entire continent, only a few countries excepted, was composed of European colonies or protectorates. Great Britain, France, Germany, Portugal, Spain, and Italy all had seized pieces of what King Leopold II of Belgium—who kept an enormous slice for himself—called "this magnificent African cake." The Scramble for Africa redrew the map, enriched Europe, and left tens of millions of Africans dead in its wake. But this history is glaringly absent from the work of first-rank European novelists of the day. It would be as if no major nineteenth-century American writer dealt with slavery, or no major twentieth-century German wrote about the Holocaust. Joseph Conrad is a rare and brave exception.

The multilayered richness of *Heart of Darkness* has made it probably the most widely read short novel in English, and certainly the most written about. If the pages of all the monograph chapters, scholarly articles, entire books, conference papers, and dissertations about *Heart of Darkness* were laid end to end, they would stretch, it seems, the full length of the Congo River and back again.

Several curious tensions run throughout the book. One is between the way the story is painfully rooted in the six grueling months that Conrad spent in the Congo, nearly dying from dysentery and malaria, and the manner in which the novel is written, where no place—indeed, almost no person—is even named. Not only the Congo but even the very continent of Africa is never mentioned as the scene of the action. And although the shape of the "great river" up which Conrad's alter ego Marlow begins steaming suggests the Congo River—"resembling an immense snake uncoiled, with its head in the sea, its body at rest curving afar over a vast country, and its tail lost in the depths of the land"—it, too, is never named. The key settings (the Central Station, the Inner Station) and most of the people Marlow meets (the manager, the Accountant, the brickmaker, the helmsman) also have no proper names.

This technique, imitated by other writers since Conrad, is certainly one source of the book's haunting power. We feel that we are reading a parable, a fable, something freighted with mythic overtones. After all, what do the snake and "traveling back to the earliest beginnings of the world" conjure up if not the Garden of Eden? For this is a book about the end of innocence and the discovery of evil. Written on the very eve of the twentieth century, the novel portrays a façade of benevolence and glory underlain by hideous brutality that seems to look forward, in a way few other writers of Conrad's time did, to the era of Auschwitz and the Soviet gulag.

It is often said that there were two great totalitarian systems of the last century, Nazism and Communism. But we too often ignore a third: European colonialism, particularly as practiced in Africa, where it could be just as brutal and as deadly as the other systems. Hitler's top deputy, Hermann Göring, sentenced to death at Nuremberg for his role in the murder of Europe's Jews, was the son of the colonial governor of German South-West Africa (today's Namibia), where the authorities carried out a deliberate genocide against the Herero people who had rebelled against German rule. And, as late as the 1950s, the British imprisoned tens of thousands of Kenyans in harsh concentration camps, in the course of ruthlessly suppressing an anticolonial revolt. The list is far longer.

For many decades, most critics and readers in the West preferred to look at *Heart of Darkness* only for what it says about the eternal human condition, rather than to consider it also as a portrait of a particular time and place. In several of its transformations into film, it has been moved completely out of Africa. The director Manuel Gutiérrez Aragón transplanted it to Spain after the Spanish Civil War in the film *El corazón del bosque (The Heart of the Forest)*. And Francis Ford Coppola moved the story to Vietnam in his *Apocalypse Now*. In part these geographical leaps are testimony to the novel's power and universality. But there is also something odd about pulling it loose from its historical moorings. Would we not think it strangely evasive if a director filmed Alexander Solzhenitsyn's *One Day in the Life of Ivan Denisovich* but didn't set it in the Soviet Union, or brought to the screen Elie Wiesel's *Night* but moved the story out of Auschwitz?

What, then, was going on in the Congo at the time Conrad went there that Europeans and Americans for so many years afterward preferred not to confront?

The colony in which an unsuspecting Conrad arrived in 1890 was in the early stages of what would be the bloodiest single chapter of the Scramble for Africa. Orchestrating it was Leopold II, the man whose formal title was the name of Conrad's steamboat: King of the Belgians. Brilliant and charming, ruthless and avaricious, a public relations genius who cloaked his greed in the rhetoric of Christian philanthropy, Leopold was openly frustrated with being king of such a small country. "*Petit pays, petit gens,*" he once said: "small country, small-minded people." Moreover, he reigned at a time when European monarchs were rapidly losing power to the electorate. And, so, he wanted a colony where he could rule supreme. The Belgian cabinet was not interested, thinking colonies an extravagance for a small country with no navy or merchant marine, but that suited Leopold perfectly: he set off to acquire his own.

To begin with, the king hired the famous explorer Henry Morton Stanley to navigate and reconnoiter the Congo River and its tributaries for him. Next, he lobbied first the United States and then all the major nations of Europe into recognizing the Congo— a vast territory more than seventy times the size of Belgium— as belonging to him *personally*. He proclaimed himself its "King-Sovereign" in 1885. It was the world's only privately owned colony.

In the early years of the Congo Free State, as Leopold inaccurately christened his new domain, the main commodity he coveted was ivory. Elephant tusks were highly prized because they could be easily carved into a wide variety of shapes: piano keys, statuettes, jewelry, false teeth, and more. The king ordered a network of ivory-gathering posts set up along the colony's riverbanks, and men who wanted to make their fortunes flocked to the Congo. As Conrad writes in *Heart of Darkness,* "The word 'ivory' rang in the air, was whispered, was sighed. You would think they were praying to it." The adventurers who headed for Leopold's new colony were often eager not just for riches but for combat. Much of the ivory was seized at gunpoint, and as Congolese resisted the foreigners who were taking over their land, there were countless rebellions to put down. For a young European or American seeking excitement, going to the Congo held the thrills of joining both a gold rush and the French Foreign Legion.

Like much of the European colonization of Africa, the entire ivory-gathering system was based on forced labor. It was forced laborers who carried the white men's supplies into the interior on their backs, forced laborers who chopped the wood that fueled the steamboats, and Congolese conscripts who were dragooned into the ranks of the king's private army. Conrad recognized Leopold's forced-labor system for what it was. Soon after Marlow, Conrad's narrator, arrives in the territory, he sees six workers on a railroad-construction crew; they "all were connected together with a chain whose bights swung between them, rhythmically clinking." Others, exhausted by their labor, have crawled into a grove of trees to die.

In the years after Conrad's visit, the toll of this forced-labor system would swell to unimaginable proportions. Although ivory remained valuable, by the late 1890s, wild rubber would supplant it as the colony's most lucrative treasure. The army went into village after village, holding the women hostage in order to force the men to go into the rain forest, for days and eventually weeks at a time, to gather a monthly quota of rubber. Many male rubber gatherers were worked to death; many women hostages starved. Tens of thousands more Congolese died in doomed uprisings against Leopold's well-armed military. Hundreds of thousands fled the forced-labor system by going deep into the rain forest, where there was little food and no shelter, and they died. And with so many Congolese turned into forced laborers, hostages, or refugees, the birth rate plummeted, and there were few able-bodied adults left to hunt, fish, or plant and harvest crops. In the resulting famine, disease took a horrendous toll among people who otherwise would have survived. From all these causes, the best estimates today are that the territory's population was slashed from somewhere around 20 million in 1880 to approximately half of that in 1920. Conrad was an eyewitness to the beginnings of one of the great human catastrophes of modern Africa.

The writer's Congo odyssey began weeks before he was able to board the *Roi des Belges*. He first set foot in the territory on June 12, 1890, when, following the long voyage from Belgium, he disembarked at the colony's capital, Boma, just inland from where the "great river" pours its enormous torrent of water—in volume second only to that of the Amazon—into the Atlantic. After a short steamer ride upstream, he set off, accompanied by one other white man and a caravan of thirty-one porters, on the arduous 230-mile trek around the succession of thundering rapids that the Congo River tumbles down on the last part of its journey from the central African plateau to the ocean. It was on this caravan route that Conrad first recorded signs of the immense violence that underlay the colony's operations. In his diary on July 3 he noted, "Met an off[ic]er of the State inspecting; a few minutes afterwards saw at a camp[in]g place the dead body of a Backongo. Shot? Horrid smell." The following day: "Saw another dead body lying by the path." And on July 29: "On the road today passed a skeleton tied up to a post."

After more than a month of walking, in shaky health, he arrived at the small trading post of Kinshasa; inland from here, it was clear sailing for steamboats for a thousand miles upstream. Only a day later Conrad was aboard the fifteen-ton *Roi des Belges*. It had been ordered to depart early by the trading company he was working for, to come to the aid of another steamer that had gotten stuck on a submerged root some distance upriver. The *Roi des Belges* passed only a half dozen other steamers during its month of traveling upstream. Typically these river steamboats would travel by daylight and then tie up onshore for the night, either at one of the militarized ivory-gathering posts where firewood for the boilers could be loaded, or sometimes just at a spot on the riverbank where the boat's crew of Congolese woodcutters could chop trees during the night for a day or two's supply of fuel.

Finally, the steamer reached Stanley Falls (today Kisangani), a settlement of ivory warehouses, army barracks, and offices for the colonial officials who controlled the eastern part of the colony. A week later, Conrad and the *Roi des Belges* headed back downstream—with the current the voyage would only take some two weeks—carrying cargo and a twenty-seven-year-old French-

man, Georges Antoine Klein, a company agent who was gravely
ill. Klein died onboard a few days before the steamer's journey
ended, a detail echoed in *Heart of Darkness*.

Some bitter disappointments punctured Conrad's Congo
dreams now that he was back in Kinshasa. He had hit it off badly
with a key company official and found that he was not slated to
take part, as he had been hoping, in an exploring expedition up
one of the Congo River's major tributaries, the Kasai. The venal-
ity and greed of the ivory hunters dismayed him. And his malaria
and dysentery, which he already had been fighting for some weeks,
grew worse, landing him in a primitive hospital at a Baptist mission station where he may have had to endure some proselytizing.
"He is a gentlemanly fellow," wrote American missionary Samuel
Lapsley in his diary. "An English [New] Testament on his table
furnishes a handle I hope to use on him." Europeans still had
few effective medicines for most tropical diseases, and roughly a
third of the white men who came to the Congo in this era died
there. Such statistics were kept concealed by King Leopold II, but
Conrad saw Klein die and surely heard of many other such deaths.
Finally, in October 1890, he decided to abandon his Africa ven-
ture and head back to Europe. On the long trip around the lower
river rapids his illness was at its worst, and he had to be carried
by porters. He arrived back in Europe early the next year, his
health permanently weakened and his view of humanity forever
darkened.

How much of what Conrad portrayed in *Heart of Darkness* was
based on his actual experience?

For most of the century after the book was written, the implicit
answer from critics was: not much, except for the superficial details of the steamboat journey up- and downriver. They analyzed
the novel in terms of Freud, Jung, and Nietzsche, of Victorian
innocence and original sin, of patriarchy and gnosticism, of post-
modernism and poststructuralism. Monographs and Ph.D. theses
poured forth with titles like "The Eye and the Gaze in 'Heart
of Darkness': A Symptomological Reading." By contrast, in a
1917 preface Conrad himself wrote, "'Heart of Darkness' is
experience . . . pushed a little (and only very little) beyond the
actual facts of the case."

There is considerable truth in what he says, and we miss much if we look at the novel *only* as a work of imaginative literature. It is also a remarkable description of "the actual facts of the case," the Scramble for Africa at its most naked. The river that Marlow travels up may never be named—and, indeed, it doesn't always physically resemble the Congo River, nor does the Inner Station much resemble the Stanley Falls Station Conrad saw. (Two recent scholars, Harry White and the late Irving L. Finston, contend that the river Conrad imagined as he wrote was the Kasai, which he had hoped to explore but never did.) But consider the figure at the novel's center, Mr. Kurtz, the brilliant, ambitious, supremely rapacious hoarder of ivory. Kurtz is sketched with only a few bold strokes, but he has become our time's most famous literary villain: the lone white man with his dreams of culture and grandeur, his great store of ivory, and his barbarous fiefdom carved out of the jungle.

No doubt Conrad drew part of Kurtz from deep within himself; that is what gives the reader a tinge of uneasy empathy with Kurtz's boundless ambition and his vision of himself as the apostle of "the cause of progress" among awestruck savages. But Conrad may also have taken aspects of Kurtz from various men whom he encountered in the Congo, or whom he heard about there or afterward.

Look, for instance, at the searing scene in which Marlow gazes from the steamboat at what he first thinks are ornamental knobs atop the fence posts near Mr. Kurtz's house. But through his binoculars he then sees that each is a human head, "black, dried, sunken, with closed eyelids." Biographers long talked of Kurtz's collection of severed heads as a brilliant example of Conrad's phantasmagoric imagination; one, Norman Sherry, even described it as possibly a "macabre transference" by Conrad of a well-known episode when an aggressive white ivory-seeker in the Congo was beheaded by African rivals.

But no macabre transference was necessary: a number of white men in the colony at this time collected African heads and openly bragged about it. One, Guillaume Van Kerckhoven, a dashing, mustachioed officer of King Leopold's private army, told a fellow steamboat passenger in 1887 that he paid his black soldiers the equivalent of two and halfpence in British money for every rebel head they brought him after a battle. "He said it was to stimulate their prowess in the face of the enemy." The man to whom Van Kerckhoven made the boast, Roger Casement, later renowned for his exposure of the brutalities of King Leopold's regime, was Conrad's housemate for some ten days in the Congo, and the two men became fast friends who later saw each other in England. Van Kerckhoven and his soldiers also traveled on the *Roi des Belges* a few months before Conrad did, so the writer could likely have heard about him from other people as well.

Another notorious head collector was an officer named Léon Fiévez, who worked in the Congo for eleven years starting in 1888. Accounts from both Africans and Europeans describe his brutal ways. To a white government agent who visited his post in 1894, Fiévez explained that when local Africans failed to supply his troops with manioc, "I made war against them. One example was enough: a hundred heads cut off, and there have been plenty of supplies at the station ever since. My goal is ultimately humanitarian. I killed a hundred people, but that allowed five hundred others to live."

We do not know whether Fiévez had yet started these "humanitarian" practices in 1890, but Conrad may have met him that year, for Fiévez had just taken command of the strategic, heavily fortified post of Basoko, a likely refueling and overnight stop for the *Roi des Belges* on its way up and down the river. Nor was it only Belgians who collected heads. One British explorer-adventurer in the Congo, part of an expedition that received a huge amount of press coverage, in 1887 packed an African's head in a box of salt and sent it to his Piccadilly taxidermist to be stuffed and mounted.

The most striking head-collector of all, with an eerie resemblance to Mr. Kurtz on several other counts as well, was a brusque-looking Congo state official named Léon Rom, whose combat exploits earned him various medals and write-ups in Belgian colonial-heroic literature of the day. When commander of the Stanley Falls station a few years after Conrad was there, Rom kept a gallows permanently erected in front of his headquarters. A British journalist who passed through in 1895 described, in the widely read *Century Magazine,* a punitive expedition Rom had mounted against African rebels: "Many women and children were taken, and twenty-one heads were brought to the falls, and have been used by Captain Rom as a decoration round a flower-bed in front of his house!"

In addition, both the real-life Rom and the fictional Kurtz carried out their looting amid pretensions to high culture. In the novel, Mr. Kurtz is an intellectual, "an emissary of . . . science and progress." Rom also had scientific ambitions: he brought many butterfly specimens back to Europe and was elected a member of the Royal Belgian Entomological Society. Furthermore, Mr. Kurtz is an artist—the painter of "a small sketch in oils" of a woman carrying a torch, which hangs on the wall of the Central Station. Léon Rom, when he was not collecting butterflies or human heads, painted portraits and landscapes, several of which can be found today in the vaults of the Royal Museum for Central Africa, outside Brussels.

Mr. Kurtz is also a writer. Among other things, he writes a seventeen-page report—"vibrating with eloquence. . . . a beautiful piece of writing" to the International Society for the Suppression of Savage Customs. Although Conrad most likely was unaware, in 1899, the same year that Heart of Darkness appeared as a magazine serial, Léon Rom fulfilled his own literary ambitions. He, too, published a report on savage customs, a jaunty, arrogant, and sweepingly superficial little book called Le Nègre du Congo. There are short chapters on "Le Nègre en Général," the black woman, food, pets, native medicine, and many pages about a particular enthusiasm of Rom's—hunting. Of "the black race," Rom says, "its feelings are coarse, its passions rough, its instincts brutish, and, in addition, it is proud and vain. . . . The black man has no idea of time, and, questioned on that subject by a European, he generally responds with something stupid."

One final notable parallel: Mr. Kurtz succeeds in "getting himself adored" by the Africans of the Inner Station. Chiefs crawl on the ground before him, the blacks obey him with slavish devotion, and a beautiful woman among them is his concubine. In 1895, a disapproving Belgian lieutenant confided to his diary a similar description of a fellow officer:

He makes his agents starve while he gives provisions in abundance to the black women of his harem. . . . Finally, he got into his dress uniform at his house, brought together his women, picked up some piece of paper and pretended to read to them that the king had named him the big chief and that the other whites of the station were only small fry. . . . He gave 50 lashes to a poor little negress because she wouldn't be his mistress, then he *gave* her to a soldier.

Significantly, the diarist introduces his account by saying, "This man wants to play the role of a second Rom."

On August 2, 1890, Conrad and Rom may have met. About five miles before reaching the riverside village of Kinshasa, where the *Roi des Belges* was waiting, he and his caravan of porters passed through the neighboring post of Léopoldville. All told, only about twenty white men were living in these two places, each of which— long before they were both absorbed into the giant metropolis today called Kinshasa—was just a scattering of thatch-roofed buildings. Léon Rom was then station chief at Leopoldville. His diary, which in a neat, almost calligraphic hand records any raid or campaign that could win him another medal, shows no expedition away from the post that day. If he was on hand, he certainly would have greeted any caravan with white newcomers, for these arrived only a few times a month. Conrad spoke near-perfect French, so they would have had a language in common.

Did Conrad meet Rom—or Fiévez or Van Kerckhoven? Did Rom tell him about his scientific, artistic, and literary ambitions, or did Conrad hear of these from others? Did Conrad see one of Rom's paintings on the wall, as Marlow does one of Kurtz's? We will never know. Nor will we ever know if any such recollections were triggered by Conrad reading the *Century Magazine*'s description of Rom's severed-head collection, which, as it happens, was also referred to in the *Saturday Review,* a magazine he admired and read faithfully, within a week or two of the day he started writing *Heart of Darkness*. But whether specific memories provided building blocks for the character of Mr. Kurtz, or whether Conrad simply worked on intuition, the novel captures something crucial about its place and time with piercing, uncanny accuracy.

*Heart of Darkness* is not always an easy book to read. There are times when the voice of Marlow seems too insistent, too extravagant—and too vague. Marlow's portrayal of Kurtz's appalling brutality seems at odds with his repeated professions of loyalty to the man. Parades of ponderous adjectives—inexorable, unspeakable, unfathomable—rumble past relentlessly. "Sentence after sentence," wrote the novelist E. M. Forster, "discharges its smoke screen into our abashed eyes." The poet John Masefield found the novel to have "too much cobweb."

What accounts for this? Clearly, when he wrote the book, Conrad was painfully wrestling with something deep within himself. Before his six months in Africa, he once told his friend the critic Edward Garnett he had had "not a thought in his head." But what he found in the Congo—dead bodies strewn about; the skeleton tied up to a post; workers in chains; an entire economy founded on the whip, the gun, and forced labor—was, he wrote in an essay published only a few months before he died, "the vilest scramble for loot that ever disfigured the history of human conscience." Some of his angst may have stemmed from embarrassment and guilt about his own youthful naïveté. He had hoped for a glamorous job skippering a steamboat on an exploring voyage—a hope which, we know from letters, persisted even into the middle of his stay in the Congo. But, as he says of Kurtz, his time there may have "whispered to him things about himself which he did not know."

There was also a political struggle going on in Conrad's soul, although he never articulated it, and never would have used that word to describe it. On one hand, he was writing the most scathing portrait of colonialism in all of Western literature. No one who reads *Heart of Darkness* can ever again imagine the colonization of central Africa as something benevolent. "To tear treasure out of the bowels of the land was their desire," Marlow says of the exploring expedition he encounters, "with no more moral purpose at the back of it than there is in burglars breaking into a safe." Nor does Conrad imply that there was anything uniquely Belgian about this burglary. Fortune-seekers in the Congo came from throughout the Western world: "All Europe contributed to the making of Kurtz." Conrad's ability to see the toll of conquest owes something to his own upbringing, for he had been born Polish at a time when Poland itself had been earlier snuffed out of existence as an independent nation, its land divided up by powerful neighbors—Prussia, Austria, and Russia. The writer spent part of his childhood in northern Russia, where his father, a Polish nationalist hero, was exiled for leading an insurrection against Russian rule.

Yet at the same time Conrad was a deeply conservative man, profoundly loyal to his adoptive country, Britain, which, of course, was the greatest colonial power of them all. Early on in the novel, when Marlow sees a map of Africa dominated by the British Empire's red and feels the color is "good to see at any time, because one knows that some real work is done in there," he is probably speaking for his creator. Indeed, Conrad once declared in a letter that "liberty . . . can only be found under the English flag all over the world."

Similarly, despite his searing portrayal of white greed, Conrad was very much a man of his own imperial time when it came to race. The Africans in this novel barely ever even speak. Instead they grunt; they chant; they produce a "drone of weird incantations" and a "wild and passionate uproar"; they spout "strings of amazing words that resembled no sounds of human language . . . like the responses of some satanic litany." *Heart of Darkness* has come in for some attacks in recent years because of this, most notably from the distinguished Nigerian novelist Chinua Achebe. But the fact that Conrad shared the attitudes of those around him about race no more disqualifies him from greatness than do Tolstoy's beliefs about the position of women or Shakespeare's about monarchy.

One final contradiction: in the middle of the decade between his six months in the Congo and the time he finally got the lust for quick riches he saw there onto paper in this novel, Conrad made an unsuccessful try at gaining quick riches himself. Although the details remain shadowy, he apparently invested and lost almost all his savings in a South African gold mine—a loss all the more embarrassing because it came just as he got married and hoped to start a family. The South African gold rush of the late 1880s and '90s was, like the simultaneous ivory and rubber boom in the Congo, one of the great bonanzas of the Scramble for Africa. Tens of thousands of miners flocked there from all over the world—as did merchants, pimps, and prostitutes, hoping to make money from them. Mine owners amassed huge fortunes.

Meanwhile, the hardest and lowest-paid manual labor was done by Africans. Pushed off their land and desperate for money to survive, they died by the thousands in underground mining accidents, were forced to leave their families behind in distant rural areas, and were deliberately provided with few recreation facilities except drinking places—which recycled much of their meager earnings back to mine owners, several of whom owned the major distillery. How much of all this was Conrad aware of? How did he feel about his failed attempt to cash in on the gold rush? We will never know, but this may be yet another of those struggles within himself which in the end only add to the depth of the book he wrote.

ADAM HOCHSCHILD

# Heart of Darkness

# I

The *Nellie*, a cruising yawl, swung to her anchor without a flutter of the sails, and was at rest. The flood had made, the wind was nearly calm, and being bound down the river, the only thing for it was to come to and wait for the turn of the tide.

The sea-reach of the Thames stretched before us like the beginning of an interminable waterway. In the offing the sea and the sky were welded together without a joint, and in the luminous space the tanned sails of the barges drifting up with the tide seemed to stand still in red clusters of canvas sharply peaked, with gleams of varnished sprits. A haze rested on the low shores that ran out to sea in vanishing flatness. The air was dark above Gravesend, and further back still seemed condensed into a mournful gloom, brooding motionless over the biggest, and the greatest, town on earth.[1]

The Director of Companies was our captain and our host. We four affectionately watched his back as he stood in the bows looking to seaward. On the whole river there was nothing that looked half so nautical. He resembled a pilot, which to a seaman is trustworthiness personified. It was difficult to realise his work was not out there in the luminous estuary, but behind him, within the brooding gloom.

Between us there was, as I have already said somewhere, the bond of the sea. Besides holding our hearts together through long periods of separation, it had the effect of making us tolerant of each other's yarns—and even convictions. The Lawyer[2]—the best of old fellows—had, because of his many years and many virtues, the only cushion on deck, and was lying on the only rug. The Accountant had brought out already a box of dominoes, and was toying architecturally with the bones. Marlow sat cross-legged right aft, leaning against the mizzenmast. He had sunken cheeks, a yellow complexion, a straight back, an ascetic aspect, and, with his arms dropped, the palms of hands outwards, resembled an idol. The Director, satisfied the anchor had good hold, made his way aft and sat down amongst us. We exchanged a few words lazily. Afterwards there was silence on board the yacht. For some reason or other we did not begin that game of dominoes. We felt meditative, and fit for nothing but placid staring. The day was ending in a serenity of still and exquisite brilliance. The water shone pacifically; the sky, without a speck, was a benign immensity of unstained light; the very mist on the Essex marshes was like a gauzy and radiant fabric, hung from the wooded rises inland, and draping the low shores in diaphanous folds.[3] Only the gloom to the west, brooding over the upper reaches, became more sombre every minute, as if angered by the approach of the sun.

And at last, in its curved and imperceptible fall, the sun sank low, and from glowing white changed to a dull red without rays and without heat, as if about to go out suddenly, stricken to death by the touch of that gloom brooding over a crowd of men.

Forthwith a change came over the waters, and the serenity became less brilliant but more profound. The old river in its broad reach rested unruffled at the decline of day, after ages of good service done to the race that peopled its banks, spread out in the tranquil dignity of a waterway leading to the uttermost ends of the earth. We looked at the venerable stream not in the vivid flush of a short day that comes and departs for ever, but in the august light of abiding memories. And indeed nothing is easier for a man who has, as the phrase goes, "followed the sea" with reverence and affection, than to evoke the great spirit of the past upon the lower reaches of the Thames. The tidal current runs to and fro in its unceasing service, crowded with memories of men and ships it had borne to the rest of home or to the battles of the sea. It had known and served all the men of whom the nation is proud, from Sir Francis Drake to Sir John Franklin, knights all, titled and untitled—the great knights-errant of the sea. It had borne all the ships whose names are like jewels flashing in the night of time, from the *Golden Hind* returning with her round flanks full of treasure, to be visited by the Queen's Highness and thus pass out of the gigantic tale, to the *Erebus* and *Terror*, bound on other conquests—and that never returned. It had known the ships and the men. They sailed from Deptford, from Greenwich, from Erith—the adventurers and the settlers; kings' ships and the ships of men on 'Change; captains, admirals, the dark "interlopers" of the Eastern trade, and the commissioned "generals" of East India fleets. Hunters for gold or pursuers of fame, they all had gone out on that stream, bearing the sword, and often the torch, messengers of the might within the land, bearers of a spark from the sacred fire. What greatness had not floated on the ebb of that river into the mystery of an unknown earth! . . . The dreams of men, the seed of commonwealths, the germs of empires.[4]

The sun set; the dusk fell on the stream, and lights began to appear along the shore. The Chapman lighthouse, a three-legged thing erect on a mudflat, shone strongly. Lights of ships moved in the fairway—a great stir of lights going up and going down. And further west on the upper reaches the place of the monstrous town was still marked ominously on the sky, a brooding gloom in sunshine, a lurid glare under the stars.

"And this also," said Marlow[5] suddenly, "has been one of the dark places of the earth."

He was the only man of us who still "followed the sea." The worst that could be said of him was that he did not represent his class. He was a seaman, but he was a wanderer too, while most seamen lead, if one may so express it, a sedentary life. Their minds are of the stay-at-home order, and their home is always with them—the ship; and so is their country—the sea. One ship is very much like another, and the sea is always the same. In the immutability of their surroundings the foreign shores, the foreign faces, the changing immensity of life, glide past, veiled not by a sense of mystery but by a slightly disdainful ignorance; for there is nothing mysterious to a seaman unless it be the sea itself, which is the mistress of his existence and as inscrutable as Destiny. For the rest, after his hours of work, a casual stroll or a casual spree on shore suffices to unfold for him the secret of a whole continent, and generally he finds the secret not worth knowing. The yarns of seamen have an effective simplicity, the whole meaning of which lies within the shell of a cracked nut. But, as has been said, Marlow was not typical (if his propensity to spin yarns be excepted), and to him the meaning of an episode was not inside like a kernel but outside,

enveloping the tale which brought it out only as a glow brings out
a haze, in the likeness of one of these misty halos that, sometimes,
are made visible by the spectral illumination of moonshine.

His remark did not seem at all surprising. It was just like Marlow. It was accepted in silence. No one took the trouble to grunt
even; and presently he said, very slow—

"I was thinking of very old times, when the Romans first came
here, nineteen hundred years ago—the other day. . . . Light came
out of this river since—you say Knights? Yes; but it is like a running blaze on a plain, like a flash of lightning in the clouds. We live
in the flicker—may it last as long as the old earth keeps rolling! But
darkness was here yesterday. Imagine the feelings of say a commander of a fine—what d'ye call 'em?—trireme in the Mediterra-
nean, ordered suddenly to the north; run overland across the Gauls
in a hurry; put in charge of one of these craft the legionaries—a
wonderful lot of handy men they must have been too—used to
build, apparently by the hundred, in a month or two, if we may
believe what we read. Imagine him here—the very end of the
world, a sea the colour of lead, a sky the colour of smoke, a kind
of ship about as rigid as a concertina—and going up this river with
stores, or orders, or what you like. Sandbanks, marshes, forests,
savages—precious little to eat fit for a civilised man, nothing but
Thames water to drink. No Falernian wine here, no going ashore.
Here and there a military camp lost in a wilderness like a needle in
a bundle of hay—cold, fog, tempests, disease, exile, and death—
death skulking in the air, in the water, in the bush. They must have
been dying like flies here. Oh yes—he did it. Did it very well, too,
no doubt, and without thinking much about it either, except afterwards to brag of what he had gone through in his time, perhaps.
They were men enough to face the darkness. And perhaps he was
cheered by keeping his eye on a chance of promotion to the fleet at
Ravenna, by and bye, if he had good friends in Rome and survived
the awful climate. Or think of a decent young citizen in a toga—
perhaps too much dice, you know—coming out here in the train
of some prefect, or tax-gatherer, or trader even, to mend his fortunes. Land in a swamp, march through the woods, and in some
inland post feel the savagery, the utter savagery, had closed round
him—all that mysterious life of the wilderness that stirs in the
forests, in the jungles, in the hearts of wild men. There's no initiation either into such mysteries. He has to live in the midst of the

incomprehensible, which is also detestable. And it has a fascination, too, that goes to work upon him. The fascination of the
abomination—you know. Imagine the growing regrets, the longing
to escape, the powerless disgust, the surrender, the hate."[6]

He paused.

"Mind," he began again, lifting one arm from the elbow, the
palm of the hand outwards, so that, with his legs folded before
him, he had the pose of a Buddha preaching in European clothes
and without a lotus-flower—"Mind, none of us would feel exactly
like this. What saves us is efficiency—the devotion to efficiency.
But these chaps were not much account, really. They were no
colonists; their administration was merely a squeeze, and nothing
more, I suspect. They were conquerors, and for that you want
only brute force—nothing to boast of, when you have it, since
your strength is just an accident arising from the weakness of others. They grabbed what they could get and for the sake of what
was to be got. It was just robbery with violence, aggravated murder on a great scale, and men going at it blind—as is very proper
for those who tackle a darkness. The conquest of the earth, which
mostly means the taking it away from those who have a different
complexion or slightly flatter noses than ourselves, is not a pretty
thing when you look into it too much.[7] What redeems it is the idea
only. An idea at the back of it; not a sentimental pretence but an
idea; and an unselfish belief in the idea—something you can set
up, and bow down before, and offer a sacrifice to. . . ."[8]

He broke off. Flames glided in on the river, small green flames,
red flames, white flames, pursuing, overtaking, joining, crossing
each other—then separating slowly or hastily. The traffic of the
great city went on in the deepening night upon the sleepless river.
We looked on, waiting patiently—there was nothing else to do till
the end of the flood; but it was only after a long silence, when he
said, in a hesitating voice, "I suppose you fellows remember I did
once turn fresh-water sailor for a bit," that we knew we were
fated, before the ebb began to run, to hear about one of Marlow's
inconclusive experiences.

"I don't want to bother you much with what happened to me
personally," he began, showing in this remark the weakness of
many tellers of tales who seem so often unaware of what their
audience would best like to hear; "yet to understand the effect of
it on me you ought to know how I got out there, what I saw, how

I went up that river to the place where I first met the poor chap. It was the furthest point of navigation and the culminating point of my experience. It seemed somehow to throw a kind of light on everything about me—and into my thoughts. It was sombre enough too—and pitiful—not extraordinary in any way—not very clear either. No, not very clear. And yet it seemed to throw a kind of light.

"I had then, as you remember, just returned to London after a lot of Indian Ocean, Pacific, China Seas—a regular dose of the East—six years or so, and I was loafing about, hindering you fellows in your work and invading your homes, just as though I had got a heavenly mission to civilise you. It was very fine for a time, but after a bit I did get tired of resting. Then I began to look for a ship—I should think the hardest work on earth. But the ships wouldn't even look at me. And I got tired of that game too.

"Now when I was a little chap I had a passion for maps. I would look for hours at South America, or Africa, or Australia and lose myself in all the glories of exploration. At that time there were many blank spaces on the earth, and when I saw one that looked particularly inviting on a map (but they all look that) I would put my finger on it and say, When I grow up I will go there. The North Pole was one of these places, I remember. Well, I haven't been there yet, and shall not try now. The glamour's off. Other places were scattered about the Equator, and in every sort of latitude all over the two hemispheres. I have been in some of them, and . . . well, we won't talk about that.⁹ But there was one yet—the biggest, the most blank, so to speak—that I had a hankering after.

"True, by this time it was not a blank space any more. It had got filled since my boyhood with rivers and lakes and names. It had ceased to be a blank space of delightful mystery—a white patch for a boy to dream gloriously over. It had become a place of darkness. But there was in it one river especially, a mighty big river, that you could see on the map, resembling an immense snake uncoiled, with its head in the sea, its body at rest curving afar over a vast country, and its tail lost in the depths of the land. And as I looked at the map of it in a shop-window, it fascinated me like a snake would a bird—a silly little bird. Then I remembered there was a big concern, a Company for trade on that river. Dash it all! I thought to myself, they can't trade without using some kind of craft on that lot of fresh water—steamboats! Why shouldn't I try to get charge of one. I went on along Fleet Street,¹⁰ but could not shake off the idea. The snake had charmed me.

"You understand it was a Continental concern, that Trading society; but I have a lot of relations living on the Continent, because it's cheap and not so nasty as it looks, they say.

"I am sorry to own I began to worry them. This was already a fresh departure for me. I was not used to get things that way, you know. I always went my own road and on my own legs where I had a mind to go. I wouldn't have believed it of myself; but, then—you see—I felt somehow I must get there by hook or by crook. So I worried them. The men said 'My dear fellow,' and did nothing. Then—would you believe it?—I tried the women. I, Charlie Marlow, set the women to work—to get a job. Heavens! Well, you see, the notion drove me. I had an aunt, a dear enthusiastic soul. She wrote: 'It will be delightful. I am ready to do anything, anything for you. It is a glorious idea. I know the wife of a very high personage in the Administration, and also a man who has lots of influence with,' etc., etc. She was determined to make no end of fuss to get me appointed skipper of a river steamboat, if such was my fancy.

"I got my appointment—of course; and I got it very quick. It appears the Company had received news that one of their captains had been killed in a scuffle with the natives. This was my chance, and it made me the more anxious to go. It was only months and months afterwards, when I made the attempt to recover what was left of the body, that I heard the original quarrel arose from a misunderstanding about some hens. Yes, two black hens. Fresleven—that was the fellow's name, a Dane—thought himself wronged somehow in the bargain, so he went ashore and started to hammer the chief of the village with a stick. Oh, it didn't surprise me in the least to hear this, and at the same time to be told that Fresleven was the gentlest, quietest creature that ever walked on two legs. No doubt he was; but he had been a couple of years already out there engaged in the noble cause, you know, and he probably felt the need at last of asserting his self-respect in some way. Therefore he whacked the old nigger mercilessly, while a big crowd of his people watched him, thunderstruck, till some man—I was told the chief's son—in desperation at hearing the old chap yell, made a tentative jab with a spear at the white man—and of course it went

quite easy between the shoulder-blades. Then the whole population cleared into the forest, expecting all kinds of calamities to
happen, while, on the other hand, the steamer Fresleven com-
manded left also in a bad panic, in charge of the engineer, I believe.
Afterwards nobody seemed to trouble much about Fresleven's remains, till I got out and stepped into his shoes. I couldn't let it rest
though; but when an opportunity offered at last to meet my predecessor, the grass growing through his ribs was tall enough to hide
his bones. They were all there. The supernatural being had not
been touched after he fell. And the village was deserted, the huts
gaped black, rotting, all askew within the fallen enclosures. A ca-
lamity had come to it, sure enough. The people had vanished. Mad
terror had scattered them, men, women, and children, through the
bush, and they had never returned. What became of the hens I
don't know either. I should think the cause of progress got them,
anyhow. However, through this glorious affair I got my appointment, before I had fairly begun to hope for it.

"I flew around like mad to get ready, and before forty-eight
hours I was crossing the Channel to show myself to my employers,
and sign the contract. In a very few hours I arrived in a city that
always makes me think of a whited sepulchre. Prejudice no doubt.
I had no difficulty in finding the Company's offices. It was the
biggest thing in the town, and everybody I met was full of it. They
were going to run an over-sea empire, and make no end of coin
by trade.

"A narrow and deserted street in deep shadow, high houses,
innumerable windows with Venetian blinds, a dead silence, grass
sprouting between the stones, imposing carriage archways right
and left, immense double doors standing ponderously ajar. I
slipped through one of these cracks, went up a swept and ungar-
nished staircase, as arid as a desert, and opened the first door I
came to. Two women, one fat and the other slim, sat on straw-
bottomed chairs, knitting black wool. The slim one got up and
walked straight at me—still knitting with downcast eyes—and
only just as I began to think of getting out of her way, as you
would for a somnambulist, stood still, and looked up. Her dress
was as plain as an umbrella-cover, and she turned round without
a word and preceded me into a waiting-room. I gave my name,
and looked about. Deal table in the middle, plain chairs all round

the walls, on one end a large shining map, marked with all the colours of a rainbow. There was a vast amount of red—good to see at any time, because one knows that some real work is done in there, a deuce of a lot of blue, a little green, smears of orange, and, on the East Coast, a purple patch, to show where the jolly pioneers of progress drink the jolly lager-beer. However, I wasn't going into any of these. I was going into the yellow. Dead in the centre. And the river was there—fascinating—deadly—like a snake. Ough! A door opened, a white-haired secretarial head, but wearing a compassionate expression, appeared, and a skinny forefinger beckoned me into the sanctuary. Its light was dim, and a heavy writing-desk squatted in the middle. From behind that structure came out an impression of pale plumpness in a frockcoat. The great man himself. He was five feet six, I should judge, and had his grip on the handle-end of ever so many millions. He shook hands, I fancy, murmured vaguely, was satisfied with my French. *Bon voyage.*

"In about forty-five seconds I found myself again in the waiting-room with the compassionate secretary, who, full of desolation and sympathy, made me sign some document. I believe I undertook amongst other things not to disclose any trade secrets. Well, I am not going to.

"I began to feel slightly uneasy. You know I am not used to such ceremonies, and there was something ominous in the atmosphere. It was just as though I had been let into some conspiracy—I don't know—something not quite right; and I was glad to get out. In the outer room the two women knitted black wool feverishly. People were arriving, and the younger one was walking back and forth introducing them. The old one sat on her chair. Her flat cloth slippers were propped up on a foot-warmer, and a cat reposed on her lap. She wore a starched white affair on her head, had a wart on one cheek, and silver-rimmed spectacles hung on the tip of her nose. She glanced at me above the glasses. The swift and indifferent placidity of that look troubled me. Two youths with foolish and cheery countenances were being piloted over, and she threw at them the same quick glance of unconcerned wisdom. She seemed to know all about them and about me too. An eerie feeling came over me. She seemed uncanny and fateful. Often far away there I thought of these two, guarding the door of

Darkness, knitting black wool as for a warm pall, one introducing, introducing continuously to the unknown, the other scrutinising the cheery and foolish faces with unconcerned old eyes. *Ave!* Old knitter of black wool. *Morituri te salutant.* Not many of these she looked at ever saw her again—not half, by a long way.

"There was yet a visit to the doctor. 'A simple formality,' assured me the secretary, with an air of taking an immense part in all my sorrows. Accordingly a young chap wearing his hat over the left eyebrow, some clerk I suppose—there must have been clerks in the business, though the house was as still as a house in a city of the dead—came from somewhere up-stairs and led me forth. He was shabby and careless, with ink-stains on the sleeves of his jacket, and his cravat was large and billowy, under a chin shaped like the toe of an old boot. It was a little too early for the doctor, so I proposed a drink, and thereupon he developed a vein of joviality. As we sat over our vermouths he glorified the Company's business and by and bye I expressed casually my surprise at him not going out there. He became very cool and collected all at once. 'I am not such a fool as I look, quoth Plato to his disciples,' he said sententiously, emptied his glass with great resolution, and we rose.

"The old doctor felt my pulse, evidently thinking of something else the while. 'Good, good for there,' he mumbled, and then with a certain eagerness asked me whether I would let him measure my head. Rather surprised, I said Yes, when he produced a thing like callipers and got the dimensions back and front and every way, taking notes carefully. He was an unshaven little man in a threadbare coat like a gaberdine, with his feet in slippers, and I thought him a harmless fool. 'I always ask leave, in the interests of science,[11] to measure the crania of those going out there,' he said. 'And when they come back too?' I asked. 'Oh, I never see them,' he remarked; 'and, moreover, the changes take place inside, you know.' He smiled, as if at some quiet joke. 'So you are going out there. Famous. Interesting too.' He gave me a searching glance, and made another note. 'Ever any madness in your family?' he asked, in a matter-of-fact tone. I felt very annoyed. 'Is that question in the interests of science too?' 'It would be,' he said, without taking notice of my irritation, 'interesting for science to watch the mental changes of individuals, on the spot,[12] but . . .' 'Are you an alienist?'[13] I interrupted. 'Every doctor should be—a little,' answered that original, imperturbably. 'I have a little theory which you Messieurs who go out there must help me to prove. This is my share in the advantages my country shall reap from the possession of such a magnificent dependency. The mere wealth I leave to others. Pardon my questions, but you are the first Englishman coming under my observation . . .' I hastened to assure him I was not in the least typical. 'If I were,' said I, 'I wouldn't be talking like this with you.' 'What you say is rather profound, and probably erroneous,' he said, with a laugh. 'Avoid irritation more than exposure to the sun. *Adieu.* How do you English say, eh? Goodbye. Ah! Goodbye. *Adieu.* In the tropics one must before everything keep calm.' . . . He lifted a warning forefinger. . . . '*Du calme, du calme. Adieu.*'

"One thing more remained to do—say good-bye to my excellent aunt. I found her triumphant. I had a cup of tea—the last decent cup of tea for many, many days—and in a room that most soothingly looked just as you would expect a lady's drawing-room to look, we had a long quiet chat by the fireside. In the course of these confidences it became quite plain to me I had been represented to the wife of the high dignitary, and goodness knows to how many more people besides, as an exceptional and gifted creature—a piece of good fortune for the Company—a man you don't get hold of every day. Good heavens! and I was going to take charge of a two pence-halfpenny river-steamboat with a penny whistle attached! It appeared, however, I was also one of the Workers, with a capital—you know. Something like an emissary of light, something like a lower sort of apostle. There had been a lot of such rot let loose in print and talk just about that time, and the excellent woman, living right in the rush of all that humbug, got carried off her feet. She talked about 'weaning those ignorant millions from their horrid ways,' till, upon my word, she made me quite uncomfortable. I ventured to hint that the Company was run for profit.

"'You forget, dear Charles, that the labourer is worthy of his hire,' she said, brightly. It's queer how out of touch with truth women are! They live in a world of their own, and there had never been anything like it, and never can be. It is too beautiful altogether, and if they were to set it up it would go to pieces before the first sunset. Some confounded fact we men have been living contentedly with ever since the day of creation would start up and knock the whole thing over.

"After this I got embraced, told to wear flannel, be sure to write often, and so on—and I left. In the street—I don't know why—a queer feeling came to me that I was an impostor. Odd thing that I, who used to clear out for any part of the world at twenty-four hours' notice, with less thought than most men give to the crossing of a street, had a moment—I won't say of hesitation, but of startled pause, before this commonplace affair. The best way I can explain it to you is by saying that, for a second or two, I felt as though, instead of going to the centre of a continent, I were about to set off for the centre of the earth.[14]

"I left in a French steamer, and she called in every blamed port they have out there, for, as far as I could see, the sole purpose of landing soldiers and custom-house officers. I watched the coast. Watching a coast as it slips by the ship is like thinking about an enigma. There it is before you—smiling, frowning, inviting, grand, mean, insipid, or savage, and always mute with an air of whispering, Come and find out. This one was almost featureless, as if still in the making, with an aspect of monotonous grimness. The edge of a colossal jungle, so dark-green as to be almost black, fringed with white surf, ran straight, like a ruled line, far, far along a blue sea whose glitter was blurred by a creeping mist. The sun was fierce, the land seemed to glisten and drip with steam. Here and there greyish-whitish specks showed up, clustered inside the white surf, with a flag flying above them perhaps. Settlements—settlements, some centuries old, and still no bigger than pin-heads on the untouched expanse of their background. We pounded along, stopped, landed soldiers; went on, landed custom-house clerks to levy toll in what looked like a God-forsaken wilderness, with a tin shed and a flag-pole lost in it; landed more soldiers—to take care of the custom-house clerks, presumably. Some, I heard, got drowned in the surf; but whether they did or not, nobody seemed particularly to care. They were just flung out there, and on we went. Every day the coast looked the same, as though we had not moved; but we passed various places—trading places—with names like Gran' Bassam, Little Popo, names that seemed to belong to some sordid farce acted in front of a sinister backcloth. The idleness of a passenger, my isolation amongst all these men with whom I had no point of contact, the oily and languid sea, the uniform sombreness of the coast, seemed to keep me away from the truth of things, within the toils of a mournful and senseless delusion. The voice of the surf heard now and then was a positive pleasure, like the speech of a brother. It was something natural, that had its reason, that had a meaning. Now and then a boat from the shore gave one a momentary contact with reality. It was paddled by black fellows. You could see from afar the white of their eyeballs glistening. They shouted, sang; their bodies streamed with perspiration; they had faces like grotesque masks—these chaps; but they had bone, muscle, a wild vitality, an intense energy of movement, that was as natural and true as the surf along their coast. They wanted no excuse for being there. They were a great comfort to look at. For a time I would feel I belonged still to a world of straightforward facts; but the feeling would not last long. Something would turn up to scare it away. Once, I remember, we came upon a man-of-war anchored off the coast. There wasn't even a shed there, and she was shelling the bush. It appears the French had one of their wars going on thereabouts. Her ensign drooped limp like a rag; the muzzles of the long eight-inch guns stuck out all over the low hull; the greasy, shiny swell swung her up lazily and let her down, swaying her thin masts. In the empty immensity of earth, sky, and water, there she was, incomprehensible, firing into a continent. Pop, would go one of the eight-inch guns; a small flame would dart and vanish, a little white smoke would disappear, a tiny projectile would give a feeble screech—and nothing happened. Nothing could happen. There was a touch of insanity in the proceeding, a sense of lugubrious drollery in the sight; and it was not dissipated by somebody on board assuring me earnestly there was a camp of natives—he called them enemies!—hidden out of sight somewhere.

"We gave her her letters (I heard the men in that lonely ship were dying of fever at the rate of three a day) and went on. We called at some more places with farcical names, where the merry dance of death and trade goes on in a still and earthy atmosphere as of an overheated catacomb; all along the formless coast bordered by dangerous surf, as if Nature herself had tried to ward off intruders; in and out of rivers, streams of death in life, whose banks were rotting into mud, whose waters, thickening into slime, invaded the contorted mangroves, that seemed to writhe at us in the extremity of an impotent despair. Nowhere did we stop long enough to get a particularised impression, but the general sense of vague and oppressive wonder grew upon me. It was like a weary pilgrimage amongst hints for nightmares.

"It was upwards of thirty days before I saw the mouth of the big river. We anchored off the seat of the government. But my work would not begin till some two hundred miles further on. So as soon as I could I made a start for a place thirty miles higher up.

"I had my passage on a little sea-going steamer. Her captain was a Swede, and knowing me for a seaman, invited me on the bridge. He was a young man, lean, fair, and morose, with lanky hair and a shuffling gait. As we left the miserable little wharf, he tossed his head contemptuously at the shore. 'Been living there?' he asked. I said, 'Yes.' 'Fine lot these government chaps—are they not?' he went on, speaking English with great precision and considerable bitterness. 'It is funny what some people will do for a few francs a month. I wonder what becomes of that kind when it goes up country?' I told him I expected to see that soon. 'So-o-o!' he exclaimed. He shuffled athwart, keeping one eye ahead vigilantly. 'Don't be too sure,' he continued. 'The other day I took up a man who hanged himself on the road. He was a Swede, too.' 'Hanged himself! Why, in God's name?' I cried. He kept on looking out watchfully. 'Who knows? The sun too much for him, or the country perhaps.'

"At last we opened a reach. A rocky cliff appeared, mounds of turned-up earth by the shore, houses on a hill, others, with iron roofs, amongst a waste of excavations, or hanging to the declivity. A continuous noise of rapids above hovered over this scene of inhabited devastation. A lot of people, mostly black and naked, moved about like ants. A jetty projected into the river. A blinding sunlight drowned all this at times in a sudden recrudescence of glare. 'There's your Company's station,' said the Swede, pointing to three wooden barrack-like structures hanging on the rocky slope. 'I will send your things up. Four boxes did you say? So. Farewell.'

"I came upon a boiler wallowing in the grass, then found a path leading up the hill. It turned aside for the boulders, and also for an undersized railway-truck lying there on its back with its wheels in the air. One was off. The thing looked as dead as the carcass of some animal. I came upon more pieces of decaying machinery, a stack of rusty rails. To the left a clump of trees made a thick shade, where dark things seemed to stir feebly. I blinked, the path was steep. A horn tooted to the right, and I saw the black people run. A heavy and dull detonation shook the ground, a puff of smoke came out of the cliff, and that was all. No change appeared on the face of the rock. They were building a railway. The cliff was not in the way of anything; but this objectless blasting was all the work going on.

"A slight clinking behind me made me turn my head. Six black men advanced in a file, toiling up the path. They walked erect and slow, balancing small baskets full of earth on their heads, and the clink kept time with their footsteps. Black rags were wound round their loins, and the short ends behind wagged to and fro like tails.[15] I could see every rib, the joints of their limbs were like knots in a rope; each had an iron collar on his neck, and all were connected together with a chain whose bights swung between them, rhythmically clinking. Another report from the cliff made me think suddenly of that ship of war I had seen firing into a continent. It was the same kind of ominous voice; but these men could by no stretch of imagination be called enemies. They were called criminals, and the outraged law, like the bursting shells, had come to them, an insoluble mystery from over the sea. All the meagre breasts panted together, the violently dilated nostrils quivered, the eyes stared stonily up-hill. They passed me within six inches, without a glance, with that complete, deathlike indifference of unhappy savages.[16] Behind this raw matter one of the reclaimed, the product of the new forces at work, strolled despondently, carrying a rifle by its middle. He had a uniform jacket with one button off, and seeing a white man on the path, hoisted his weapon on to his shoulder with alacrity. This was simple prudence, white men being so much alike at a distance that he could not tell who I might be. He was speedily reassured, and with a large, white, rascally grin, and a glance at his charge, seemed to take me into partnership in his exalted trust. After all, I also was a part of the great cause of these high and just proceedings.

"Instead of going up, I turned and descended to the left. My idea was to let that chain-gang get out of sight before I climbed the hill. You know I am not particularly tender; I've had to strike and to fend off. I've had to resist and to attack sometimes—that's only one way of resisting—without counting the exact cost, according to the demands of such sort of life as I had blundered into. I've seen the devil of violence, and the devil of greed, and the devil of hot desire; but, by all the stars! these were strong, lusty, red-eyed devils, that swayed and drove men—men, I tell you. But as I stood on this hillside, I foresaw that in the blinding sunshine of that land I would become acquainted with a flabby, pretending, weak-eyed devil of a rapacious and pitiless folly. How insidious he could be, too, I was only to find out several months later and a thousand miles further. For a moment I stood appalled, as though by a warning. Finally I descended the hill, obliquely, towards the trees I had seen.

"I avoided a vast, artificial hole somebody had been digging on the slope, the purpose of which I found it impossible to divine. It wasn't a quarry or a sandpit, anyhow. It was just a hole. It might have been connected with the philanthropic desire of giving the criminals something to do. I don't know. Then I nearly fell into a very narrow ravine, almost no more than a scar in the hillside. I discovered that a lot of imported drainage-pipes for the settlement had been tumbled in there. There wasn't one that was not broken. It was a wanton smash-up. At last I got under the trees. My purpose was to stroll into the shade for a moment; but no sooner within than it seemed to me I had stepped into the gloomy circle of some Inferno. The rapids were near, and an uninterrupted, uniform, headlong, rushing noise filled the mournful stillness of the grove, where not a breath stirred, not a leaf moved, with a mysterious sound—as though the tearing pace of the launched earth had suddenly become audible.

"Black shapes crouched, lay, sat between the trees, leaning against the trunks, clinging to the earth, half coming out, half effaced within the dim light, in all the attitudes of pain, abandonment, and despair. Another mine on the cliff went off, followed by a slight shudder of the soil under my feet. The work was going on. The work! And this was the place where some of the helpers had withdrawn to die.

"They were dying slowly—it was very clear. They were not enemies, they were not criminals, they were nothing earthly now—nothing but black shadows of disease and starvation, lying confusedly in the greenish gloom. Brought from all the recesses of the coast in all the legality of time contracts, lost in uncongenial surroundings, fed on unfamiliar food, they sickened, became inefficient, and were then allowed to crawl away and rest. These moribund shapes were free as air—and nearly as thin. I began to distinguish the gleam of eyes under the trees. Then, glancing down, I saw a face near my hand. The black bones reclined at full length with one shoulder against the tree, and slowly the eyelids rose and the sunken eyes looked up at me, enormous and vacant, a kind of blind, white flicker in the depths of the orbs, which died out slowly. The man seemed young—almost a boy—but you know with them it's hard to tell. I found nothing else to do but to offer him one of my good Swede's ship's biscuits I had in my pocket. The fingers closed slowly on it and held—there was no other movement and no other glance. He had tied a bit of white worsted round his neck—Why? Where did he get it? Was it a badge—an ornament—a charm—a propitiatory act? Was there any idea at all connected with it? It looked startling round his black neck, this bit of white thread from beyond the seas.

"Near the same tree two more, bundles of acute angles, sat with their legs drawn up. One, with his chin propped on his knees, stared at nothing, in an intolerable and appalling manner: his brother phantom rested its forehead, as if overcome with a great weariness; and all about others were scattered in every pose of contorted collapse, as in some picture of a massacre or a pestilence. While I stood horror-struck, one of these creatures rose to his hands and knees, and went off on all-fours towards the river to drink. He lapped out of his hand, then sat up in the sunlight, crossing his shins in front of him, and after a time let his woolly head fall on his breastbone.

"I didn't want any more loitering in the shade, and I made haste towards the station. When near the buildings I met a white man, in such an unexpected elegance of get-up that in the first moment I took him for a sort of vision. I saw a high starched collar, white cuffs, a light alpaca jacket, snowy trousers, a clear silk necktie, and varnished boots. No hat. Hair parted, brushed, oiled, under a green-lined parasol held in a big white hand. He was amazing, and had a penholder behind his ear.

"I shook hands with this miracle, and I learned he was the Company's chief accountant, and that all the book-keeping was done at this station. He had come out for a moment, he said, 'to get a breath of fresh air.' The expression sounded wonderfully odd, with its suggestion of sedentary desk-life. I wouldn't have mentioned the fellow to you at all, only it was from his lips that I first heard the name of the man who is so indissolubly connected with the memories of that time. Moreover, I respected the fellow. Yes; I respected his collars, his vast cuffs, his brushed head. His appearance was certainly that of a hairdresser's dummy; but in the great demoralisation of the land he kept up his appearance. That's backbone! His starched collars and got-up shirt-fronts were achievements of character. He had been out nearly three years; and, later on, I could not help asking him how he managed to sport such linen. He had just the faintest blush, and said modestly, 'I've been teaching one of the native women about the station. It was difficult. She had a distaste for the work.' Thus this man had, verily, accomplished something. And he was devoted to his books, which were in apple-pie order.

"Everything else in the station was in a muddle—heads, things, buildings. Caravans, strings of dusty niggers with splay feet arrived and departed; a stream of manufactured goods, rubbishy cottons, beads, and brass wire set off into the depths of darkness, and in return came a precious trickle of ivory.

"I had to wait in this station for ten days—an eternity. I lived in a tent in the yard, but to be out of the chaos I would sometimes get into the accountant's office. It was built of horizontal planks, and so badly put together that, as he bent over his high desk, he was barred from neck to heels with narrow strips of sunlight. There was no need to open the big shutter to see. It was hot there too; big flies buzzed fiendishly, and did not sting, but stabbed. I sat generally on the floor, while, of faultless appearance (and even slightly scented), perching on a high stool, he wrote, he wrote. Sometimes he stood up for exercise. When a truckle-bed with a sick man (some invalided 'agent' from up country) was hurriedly put in there, he exhibited a gentle annoyance. 'The groans of this sick person,' he said, 'distract my attention. And without that it is extremely difficult to guard against clerical errors in this climate.'

"One day he remarked, without lifting his head, 'In the interior you will no doubt meet Mr Kurtz.' On my asking who Mr Kurtz was, he said he was a first-class agent; and seeing my disappointment at this information, he added slowly, laying down his pen, 'He is a very remarkable person.' Further questions elicited from him that Mr Kurtz was at present in charge of a trading-post, a very important one, in the true ivory-country, at 'the very bottom of there. Sends in as much ivory as all the others put together . . .' He began to write again. The sick man was too ill to groan. The flies buzzed in a great peace.

"Suddenly there was a growing murmur of voices and a great tramping of feet. A caravan had come in. A violent babble of uncouth sounds burst out on the other side of the planks. All the carriers were speaking together, and in the midst of the uproar the lamentable voice of the chief agent was heard 'giving it up' tearfully for the twentieth time that day. . . . He rose slowly. 'What a frightful row,' he said. He crossed the room gently to look at the sick man, and returning, said to me, 'He does not hear.' 'What! Dead?' I asked, startled. 'No, not yet,' he answered, with great composure. Then, alluding with a toss of the head to the tumult in the station-yard, 'When one has got to make correct entries, one comes to hate these savages—hate them to the death!' He remained thoughtful for a moment. 'When you see Mr Kurtz,' he went on, 'tell him from me that everything here'—he glanced at the desk—'is very satisfactory. I don't like to write to him—with those messengers of ours you never know who may get hold of your letter—at that Central Station.' He stared at me for a moment with his mild, bulging eyes. 'Oh, he will go far, very far,' he began again. 'He will be a somebody in the Administration before long. They, above—the Council in Europe, you know—mean him to be.'

"He turned to his work. The noise outside had ceased, and presently in going out I stopped at the door. In the steady buzz of flies the homeward-bound agent was lying flushed and insensible; the other, bent over his books, was making correct entries of perfectly correct transactions; and fifty feet below the doorstep I could see the still tree-tops of the grove of death.

"Next day I left that station at last, with a caravan of sixty men, for a two-hundred-mile tramp.

"No use telling you much about that. Paths, paths, everywhere; a stamped-in network of paths spreading over an empty land, through long grass, through burnt grass, through thickets, down and up chilly ravines, up and down stony hills ablaze with heat; and a solitude, a solitude, nobody, not a hut. The population had cleared out a long time ago. Well, if a lot of mysterious niggers armed with all kinds of fearful weapons suddenly took to travelling on the road between Deal and Gravesend, catching the yokels right and left to carry heavy loads for them, I fancy every farm and cottage thereabouts would get empty very soon. Only here the dwellings were gone too. Still I passed through several abandoned villages. There's something pathetically childish in the ruins of grass walls. Day after day, with the stamp and shuffle of sixty pair of bare feet behind me, each pair under a sixty-pound load. Camp, cook, sleep, strike camp, march. Now and then a carrier dead in harness, at rest in the long grass near the path, with an empty water-gourd and his long staff lying by his side. A great silence around and above. Perhaps on some quiet night the tremor of far-off drums, sinking, swelling, a tremor vast, faint; a sound weird, appealing, suggestive, and wild—and perhaps with as profound a meaning as the sound of bells in a Christian country. Once a white man in an unbuttoned uniform, camping on the path with an armed escort of lank Zanzibaris, very hospitable and festive—not to say drunk. Was looking after the upkeep of the road, he declared. Can't say I saw any road or any upkeep, unless the body of a middle-aged negro, with a bullet-hole in the forehead, upon which I absolutely stumbled three miles further on, may be considered as a permanent improvement. I had a white companion too, not a bad chap, but rather too fleshy and with the exasperating habit of fainting on the hot hillsides, miles away from the least bit of shade and water. Annoying, you know, to hold your own coat like a parasol over a man's head while he is coming-to. I couldn't help asking him once what he meant by coming there at all. 'To make money, of course.[17] What do you think?' he said, scornfully. Then he got fever, and had to be carried in a hammock slung under a pole. As he weighed sixteen stone I had no end of rows with the carriers. They jibbed, ran away, sneaked off with their loads in the night—quite a mutiny. So, one evening, I made a speech in English with gestures, not one of which was lost to the sixty pairs of eyes before me, and the next morning I started the hammock off in front all right. An hour afterwards I came upon the whole concern wrecked in a bush—

man, hammock, groans, blankets, horrors. The heavy pole had skinned his poor nose. He was very anxious for me to kill somebody, but there wasn't the shadow of a carrier near. I remembered the old doctor—'It would be interesting for science to watch the mental changes of individuals, on the spot.' I felt I was becoming scientifically interesting. However, all that is to no purpose. On the fifteenth day I came in sight of the big river again, and hobbled into the Central Station. It was on a back water surrounded by scrub and forest, with a pretty border of smelly mud on one side, and on the three others enclosed by a crazy fence of rushes. A neglected gap was all the gate it had, and the first glance at the place was enough to let you see the flabby devil was running that show. White men with long staves in their hands appeared languidly from amongst the buildings, strolling up to take a look at me, and then retired out of sight somewhere. One of them, a stout, excitable chap with black moustaches, informed me with great volubility and many digressions, as soon as I told him who I was, that my steamer was at the bottom of the river. I was thunderstruck. What, how, why? Oh, it was 'all right.' The 'manager himself' was there. All quite correct. 'Everybody had behaved splendidly! splendidly!'—'you must,' he said in agitation, 'go and see the general manager at once. He is waiting!'

"I did not see the real significance of that wreck at once. I fancy I see it now, but I am not sure—not at all. Certainly the affair was too stupid—when I think of it—to be altogether natural. Still . . . But at the moment it presented itself simply as a confounded nuisance. The steamer was sunk. They had started two days before in a sudden hurry up the river with the manager on board, in charge of some volunteer skipper, and before they had been out three hours they tore the bottom out of her on stones, and she sank near the south bank. I asked myself what I was to do there, now my boat was lost. As a matter of fact, I had plenty to do in fishing my command out of the river. I had to set about it the very next day. That, and the repairs when I brought the pieces to the station, took some months.

"My first interview with the manager was curious. He did not ask me to sit down after my twenty-mile walk that morning. He was commonplace in complexion, in feature, in manner, and in voice.[18] He was of middle size and of ordinary build. His eyes, of the usual blue, were perhaps remarkably cold, and he certainly

could make his glance fall on one as trenchant and heavy as an
axe. But even at these times the rest of his person seemed to dis-
claim the intention. Otherwise there was only an indefinable,
faint expression of his lips, something stealthy—a smile—not a
smile—I remember it, but I can't explain. It was unconscious, this
smile was, though just after he had said something it got intensified for an instant.[19] It came at the end of his speeches like a seal
applied on the words to make the meaning of the commonest
phrase appear absolutely inscrutable. He was a common trader,
from his youth up employed in these parts—nothing more. He
was obeyed, yet he inspired neither love nor fear, nor even respect.
He inspired uneasiness. That was it! Uneasiness. Not a definite
mistrust—just uneasiness—nothing more. You have no idea how
effective such a . . . a . . . faculty can be. He had no genius for
organising, for initiative, or for order even. That was evident in
such things as the deplorable state of the station. He had no learning, and no intelligence. His position had come to him—why?
Perhaps because he was never ill . . . He had served three terms of
three years out there . . . Because triumphant health in the general
rout of constitutions is a kind of power in itself. When he went
home on leave he rioted on a large scale—pompously. Jack
ashore—with a difference—in externals only. This one could
gather from his casual talk. He originated nothing, he could keep
the routine going—that's all. But he was great. He was great by
this little thing that it was impossible to tell what could control
such a man. He never gave that secret away. Perhaps there was
nothing within him. Such a suspicion made one pause—for out
there there were no external checks. Once when various tropical
diseases had laid low almost every 'agent' in the station, he was
heard to say, 'Men who come out here should have no entrails.'
He sealed the utterance with that smile of his, as though it had
been a door opening into a darkness he had in his keeping. You
fancied you had seen things—but the seal was on. When annoyed
at meal-times by the constant quarrels of the white men about
precedence, he ordered an immense round table to be made, for
which a special house had to be built. This was the station's mess-
room. Where he sat was the first place—the rest were nowhere.
One felt this to be his unalterable conviction.[20] He was neither
civil nor uncivil. He was quiet. He allowed his 'boy'—an overfed

young negro from the coast—to treat the white men, under his very eyes, with provoking insolence.

"He began to speak as soon as he saw me. I had been very long on the road. He could not wait. Had to start without me. The up-river stations had to be relieved. There had been so many delays already that he did not know who was dead and who was alive, and how they got on—and so on, and so on. He paid no attention to my explanations, and, playing with a stick of sealing-wax, repeated several times that the situation was 'very grave, very grave.' There were rumours that a very important station was in jeopardy, and its chief, Mr Kurtz, was ill. Hoped it was not true. Mr Kurtz was . . . I felt weary and irritable. Hang Kurtz, I thought. I interrupted him by saying I had heard of Mr Kurtz on the coast. 'Ah! So they talk of him down there,' he murmured to himself. Then he began again, assuring me Mr Kurtz was the best agent he had, an exceptional man, of the greatest importance to the Company; therefore I could understand his anxiety. He was, he said, 'very, very uneasy.' Certainly he fidgeted on his chair a good deal, exclaimed, 'Ah, Mr Kurtz!', broke the stick of sealing-wax and seemed dumbfounded by the accident. Next thing he wanted to know 'how long it would take to—' I interrupted him again. Being hungry, you know, and kept on my feet too, I was getting savage. 'How could I tell?' I said. 'I hadn't even seen the wreck yet—some months, no doubt.' All this talk seemed to me so futile. 'Some months,' he said. 'Well, let us say three months before we can make a start. Yes. That ought to do the affair.' I flung out of his hut (he lived all alone in a clay hut with a sort of verandah) muttering to myself my opinion of him. He was a chattering idiot. Afterwards I took it back when it was borne upon me startlingly with what extreme nicety he had estimated the time requisite for the 'affair.'

"I went to work the next day, turning, so to speak, my back on that station. In that way only it seemed to me I could keep my hold on the redeeming facts of life. Still, one must look about sometimes; and then I saw this station, these men strolling aimlessly about in the sunshine of the yard. I asked myself sometimes what it all meant. They wandered here and there with their absurd long staves in their hands, like a lot of faithless pilgrims bewitched inside a rotten fence. The word 'ivory' rang in the air, was whispered, was sighed. You would think they were praying to it. A taint of imbecile rapacity blew through it all, like a whiff from some corpse. By Jove! I've never seen anything so unreal in my life. And outside, the silent wilderness surrounding this cleared speck on the earth struck me as something great and invincible, like evil or truth, waiting patiently for the passing away of this fantastic invasion.

"Oh, these months! Well, never mind. Various things happened. One evening a grass shed full of calico, cotton prints, beads, and I don't know what else, burst into a blaze so suddenly that you would have thought the earth had opened to let an avenging fire consume all that trash. I was smoking my pipe quietly by my dismantled steamer, and saw them all cutting capers in the light, with their arms lifted high, when the stout man with moustaches came tearing down to the river, a tin pail in his hand, assured me that everybody was 'behaving splendidly, splendidly,' dipped about a quart of water and tore back again. I noticed there was a hole in the bottom of his pail.

"I strolled up. There was no hurry. You see the thing had gone off like a box of matches. It had been hopeless from the very first. The flame had leaped high, driven everybody back, lighted up everything—and collapsed. The shed was already a heap of embers glowing fiercely. A nigger was being beaten near by. They said he had caused the fire in some way; be that as it may, he was screeching most horribly. I saw him, later on, for several days, sitting in a bit of shade looking very sick and trying to recover himself: afterwards he arose and went out—and the wilderness without a sound took him into its bosom again. As I approached the glow from the dark I found myself at the back of two men, talking. I heard the name of Kurtz pronounced, then the words, 'take advantage of this unfortunate accident.' One of the men was the manager. I wished him a good evening. 'Did you ever see anything like it—eh? it is incredible,' he said, and walked off. The other man remained. He was a first-class agent, young, gentlemanly, a bit reserved, with a forked little beard and a hooked nose. He was stand-offish with the other agents, and they on their side said he was the manager's spy upon them. As to me, I had hardly ever spoken to him before. We got into talk, and by and bye we strolled away from the hissing ruins. Then he asked me to his room, which was in the main building of the station. He struck a match, and I perceived that this young aristocrat had not only a silver-mounted dressing-case but also a whole candle all to himself. Just at that time the manager was the only man supposed to have any right to candles. Native mats covered the clay walls; a collection of spears, assegais, shields, knives was hung up in trophies. The business entrusted to this fellow was the making of bricks—so I had been informed; but there wasn't a fragment of a brick anywhere in the station, and he had been there more than a year—waiting. It seems he could not make bricks without something, I don't know what—straw maybe. Anyway, it could not be found there, and as it was not likely to be sent from Europe, it did not appear clear to me what he was waiting for. An act of special creation perhaps. However, they were all waiting—all the sixteen or twenty pilgrims of them—for something; and upon my word it did not seem an uncongenial occupation, from the way they took it, though the only thing that ever came to them was disease—as far as I could see. They beguiled the time by backbiting and intriguing against each other in a foolish kind of way. There was an air of plotting about that station, but nothing came of it, of course. It was as unreal as everything else—as the philanthropic pretence of the whole concern, as their talk, as their government, as their show of work. The only real feeling was a desire to get appointed to a trading-post where ivory was to be had, so that they could earn percentages. They intrigued and slandered and hated each other only on that account—but as to effectually lifting a little finger—oh, no. By heavens! there is something after all in the world allowing one man to steal a horse while another must not look at a halter. Steal a horse straight out. Very well. He has done it. Perhaps he can ride. But there is a way of looking at a halter that would provoke the most charitable of saints into a kick.

"I had no idea why he wanted to be so sociable, but as we chatted in there it suddenly occurred to me the fellow was trying to get at something—in fact, pumping me. He alluded constantly to Europe, to the people I was supposed to know there—putting leading questions as to my acquaintances in the sepulchral city, and so on. His little eyes glittered like mica discs—with curiosity—though he tried to keep up a bit of superciliousness. At first I was astonished, but very soon I became also awfully curious to see what he would find out from me. I couldn't possibly imagine what I had in me to make it worth his while. It was very pretty to see how he baffled himself, for in truth my body was full of chills, and my head had nothing in it but that wretched steamboat busi-

ness. It was evident he took me for a perfectly shameless prevari-
cator. At last he got angry, and, to conceal a movement of furious
annoyance, he yawned. I rose. Then I noticed a small sketch in
oils, on a panel, representing a woman, draped and blindfolded,
carrying a lighted torch. The background was sombre—almost
black. The movement of the woman was stately, and the effect of
the torchlight on the face was sinister.

"It arrested me, and he stood by, civilly holding an empty half-
pint champagne bottle (medical comforts) with the candle stuck
in it. To my question he said Mr Kurtz had painted this—in this
very station more than a year ago—while waiting for means to go
to his trading-post. 'Tell me, pray,' said I, 'who is this Mr Kurtz?'

"'The chief of the Inner Station,' he answered in a short tone,
looking away. 'Much obliged,' I said, laughing. 'And you are the
brickmaker of the Central Station. Every one knows that.' He was
silent for a while. 'He is a prodigy,' he said at last. 'He is an emissary of pity, and science, and progress, and devil knows what else.
We want,' he began to declaim suddenly, 'for the guidance of the
cause entrusted to us by Europe, so to speak, higher intelligence,
wide sympathies, a singleness of purpose.' 'Who says that?' I
asked. 'Lots of them,' he replied. 'Some even write that; and so *he*
comes here, a special being, as you ought to know.' 'Why ought I
to know?' I interrupted, really surprised. He paid no attention.
'Yes. To-day he is chief of the best station, next year he will be
assistant-manager, two years more and . . . but I daresay you
know what he will be in two years' time. You are of the new
gang—the gang of virtue. The same people who sent him specially
also recommended you. Oh, don't say no. I've my own eyes to
trust.' Light dawned upon me. My dear aunt's influential acquaintances were producing an unexpected effect upon that young
man. I nearly burst into a laugh. 'Do you read the Company's
confidential correspondence?' I asked. He hadn't a word to say. It
was great fun. 'When Mr Kurtz,' I continued severely, 'is General
Manager, you won't have the opportunity.'

"He blew the candle out suddenly, and we went outside. The
moon had risen. Black figures strolled about listlessly, pouring
water on the glow, whence proceeded a sound of hissing; steam
ascended in the moonlight, the beaten nigger groaned somewhere.
'What a row the brute makes!' said the indefatigable man with the

moustaches, appearing near us. 'Serve him right. Transgression—
punishment—bang! Pitiless, pitiless. That's the only way. This
will prevent all conflagrations for the future. I was just telling the
manager . . .' He noticed my companion, and became crestfallen
all at once. 'Not in bed yet,' he said, with a kind of servile heart-
iness; 'it's so natural. Ha! Danger—agitation.' He vanished. I
went on to the river-side, and the other followed me. I heard a
scathing murmur at my ear, 'Heap of muffs—go to.' The pilgrims
could be seen in knots gesticulating, discussing. Several had still
their staves in their hands. I verily believe they took these sticks
to bed with them. Beyond the fence the forest stood up spectrally²¹
in the moonlight, and through the dim stir, through the faint
sounds of that lamentable courtyard, the silence of the land went
home to one's very heart—its mystery, its greatness, the amazing
reality of its concealed life. The hurt nigger moaned feebly somewhere near by, and then fetched a deep sigh that made me mend
my pace away from there. I felt a hand introducing itself under my
arm. 'My dear sir,' said the fellow, 'I don't want to be misunder-
stood, and especially by you, who will see Mr Kurtz long before
I can have that pleasure. I wouldn't like him to get a false idea of
my disposition. . . .'

  "I let him run on, this papier-mâché Mephistopheles, and it
seemed to me that if I tried I could poke my forefinger through
him, and find nothing inside but a little loose dirt, maybe. He,
don't you see, had been planning to be assistant-manager by and
bye under the present man, and I could see that the coming of that
Kurtz had upset them both not a little. He talked precipitately,
and I did not try to stop him. I had my shoulders against the
wreck of my steamer, hauled up on the slope like a carcass of
some big river animal. The smell of mud, of primeval mud, by
Jove! was in my nostrils, the high stillness of primeval forests was
before my eyes; there were shiny patches on the black creek. The
moon had spread over everything a thin layer of silver—over the
rank grass, over the mud, upon the wall of matted vegetation
standing higher than the wall of a temple, over the great river I
could see through a sombre gap glittering, glittering, as it flowed
broadly by without a murmur. All this was great, expectant,
mute, while the man jabbered about himself. I wondered whether
the stillness on the face of the immensity looking at us two were

meant as an appeal or as a menace. What were we who had strayed in here? Could we handle that dumb thing, or would it handle us? I felt how big, how confoundedly big, was that thing that couldn't talk, and perhaps was deaf as well. What was in there? I could see a little ivory coming out from there, and I had heard Mr Kurtz was in there. I had heard enough about it too—God knows! Yet somehow it didn't bring any image with it—no more than if I had been told an angel or a fiend was in there. I believed it in the same way one of you might believe there are inhabitants in the planet Mars. I knew once a Scotch sailmaker who was certain, dead sure, there were people in Mars. If you asked him for some idea how they looked and behaved, he would get shy and mutter something about 'walking on all-fours.' If you as much as smiled, he would—though a man of sixty—offer to fight you. I would not have gone so far as to fight for Kurtz, but I went for him near enough to a lie. You know I hate, detest, and can't bear a lie, not because I am straighter than the rest of us, but simply because it appals me. There is a taint of death, a flavour of mortality in lies—which is exactly what I hate and detest in the world—what I want to forget. It makes me miserable and sick, like biting something rotten would do. Temperament, I suppose. Well, I went near enough to it by letting the young fool there be- lieve anything he liked to imagine as to my influence in Europe. I became in an instant as much of a pretence as the rest of the be- witched pilgrims. This simply because I had a notion it somehow would be of help to that Kurtz whom at the time I did not see— you understand. He was just a word for me. I did not see the man in the name any more than you do.[22] Do you see him? Do you see the story? Do you see anything? It seems to me I am trying to tell you a dream—making a vain attempt, because no relation of a dream can convey the dream-sensation, that commingling of ab- surdity, surprise, and bewilderment in a tremor of struggling re- volt, that notion of being captured by the incredible which is of the very essence of dreams. . . ."

He was silent for a while.

". . . No, it is impossible; it is impossible to convey the life- sensation of any given epoch of one's existence—that which makes its truth, its meaning—its subtle and penetrating essence. It is impossible. We live, as we dream—alone. . . ."

He paused again as if reflecting, then added—

"Of course in this you fellows see more than I could then. You see me, whom you know. . . ."

It had become so pitch dark that we listeners could hardly see one another. For a long time already he, sitting apart, had been no more to us than a voice. There was not a word from anybody. The others might have been asleep, but I was awake. I listened, I listened on the watch for the sentence, for the word, that would give me the clue to the faint uneasiness inspired by this narrative that seemed to shape itself without human lips in the heavy night-air of the river.

". . . Yes—I let him run on," Marlow began again, "and think what he pleased about the powers that were behind me. I did! And there was nothing behind me! There was nothing but that wretched, old, mangled steamboat I was leaning against, while he talked fluently about 'the necessity for every man to get on.' 'And when one comes out here, you conceive, it is not to gaze at the moon.' Mr Kurtz was a 'universal genius,' but even a genius would find it easier to work with 'adequate tools—intelligent men.' He did not make bricks—why, there was a physical impossibility in the way—as I was well aware; and if he did secretarial work for the manager, it was because 'no sensible man rejects wantonly the confidence of his superiors.' Did I see it? I saw it. What more did I want? What I really wanted was rivets, by heaven! Rivets. To get on with the work—to stop the hole.²³ Rivets I wanted. There were cases of them down at the coast—cases—piled up—burst—split! You kicked a loose rivet at every second step in that station yard on the hillside. Rivets had rolled into the grove of death. You could fill your pockets with rivets for the trouble of stooping down—and there wasn't one rivet to be found where it was wanted. We had plates that would do, but nothing to fasten them with. And every week the messenger, a lone negro, letter-bag on shoulder and staff in hand, left our station for the coast. And several times a week a coast caravan came in with trade goods— ghastly glazed calico that made you shudder only to look at it, glass beads value about a penny a quart, confounded spotted cotton handkerchiefs. And no rivets. Three carriers could have brought all that was wanted to set that steamboat afloat.

"He was becoming confidential now, but I fancy my unrespon-sive attitude must have exasperated him at last, for he judged it necessary to inform me he feared neither God nor devil, let alone any mere man. I said I could see that very well, but what I wanted was a certain quantity of rivets—and rivets were what really Mr Kurtz wanted, if he had only known it. Now letters went to the coast every week. . . . 'My dear sir,' he cried, 'I write from dictation.' I demanded rivets. There was a way—for an intelligent man. He changed his manner; became very cold, and suddenly began to talk about a hippopotamus; wondered whether sleeping on board the steamer (I stuck to my salvage night and day) I wasn't disturbed. There was an old hippo that had the bad habit of getting out on the bank and roaming at night over the station grounds. The pilgrims used to turn out in a body and empty every rifle they could lay hands on at him. Some even had sat up o' nights for him. All this energy was wasted, though. 'That animal has a charmed life,' he said; 'but you can say this only of brutes in this country. No man—you apprehend me?—no man here bears a charmed life.' He stood there for a moment in the moonlight with his delicate hooked nose set a little askew, and his mica eyes glittering without a wink, then, with a curt Good night, he strode off. I could see he was disturbed and considerably puzzled, which made me feel more hopeful than I had been for days. It was a great comfort to turn from that chap to my influential friend, the battered, twisted, ruined, tin-pot steamboat. I clambered on board. She rang under my feet like an empty Huntley & Palmers biscuit-tin kicked along a gutter; she was nothing so solid in make, and rather less pretty in shape, but I had expended enough hard work on her to make me love her. No influential friend would have served me better. She had given me a chance to come out a bit—to find out what I could do. No, I don't like work. I had rather laze about and think of all the fine things that can be done. I don't like work—no man does—but I like what is in the work—the chance to find yourself. Your own reality—for yourself, not for others—what no other man can ever know. They can only see the mere show, and never can tell what it really means.

"I was not surprised to see somebody sitting aft, on the deck, with his legs dangling over the mud. You see I rather chummed with the few mechanics there were in that station, whom the other pilgrims naturally despised—on account of their imperfect manners, I suppose. This was the foreman—a boiler-maker by trade—a good worker. He was a lank, bony, yellow-faced man, with big

intense eyes. His aspect was worried, and his head was as bald as
the palm of my hand; but his hair in falling seemed to have stuck
to his chin, and had prospered in the new locality, for his beard
hung down to his waist. He was a widower with six young children (he had left them in charge of a sister of his to come out
there), and the passion of his life was pigeon-flying. He was an
enthusiast and a connoisseur. He would rave about pigeons. After
work hours he used sometimes to come over from his hut for a
talk about his children and his pigeons; at work, when he had to
crawl in the mud under the bottom of the steamboat, he would tie
up that beard of his in a kind of white serviette he brought for the
purpose. It had loops to go over his ears. In the evening he could
be seen squatted on the bank rinsing that wrapper in the creek
with great care, then spreading it solemnly on a bush to dry.

"I slapped him on the back and shouted, 'We shall have rivets!'
He scrambled to his feet exclaiming, 'No! Rivets!' as though he
couldn't believe his ears. Then in a low voice, 'You . . . eh?' I don't
know why we behaved like lunatics. I put my finger to the side of
my nose and nodded mysteriously. 'Good for you!' he cried,
snapped his fingers above his head, lifting one foot. I tried a jig.
We capered on the iron deck. A frightful clatter came out of that
empty hulk, and the virgin forest on the other bank of the creek
sent it back in a thundering roll upon the sleeping station. It must
have made some of the pilgrims sit up in their hovels. A dark figure obscured the lighted doorway of the manager's hut, vanished,
then, a second or so after, the doorway itself vanished too. We
stopped, and the silence driven away by the stamping of our feet
flowed back again from the recesses of the land. The great wall of
vegetation, an exuberant and entangled mass of trunks, branches,
leaves, boughs, festoons, motionless in the moonlight, was like a
rioting invasion of soundless life, a rolling wave of plants, piled
up, crested, ready to topple over the creek, to sweep every little
man of us out of his little existence.[24] And it moved not. A dead-
ened burst of mighty splashes and snorts reached us from afar, as
though an ichthyosaurus had been taking a bath of glitter in the
great river. 'After all,' said the boiler-maker in a reasonable tone,
'why shouldn't we get the rivets?' Why not, indeed! I did not
know of any reason why we shouldn't. 'They'll come in three
weeks,' I said, confidently.

"But they didn't. Instead of rivets there came an invasion, an
infliction, a visitation.²⁵ It came in sections during the next three
weeks, each section headed by a donkey carrying a white man in
new clothes and tan shoes, bowing from that elevation right and
left to the impressed pilgrims. A quarrelsome band of footsore
sulky niggers trod on the heels of the donkey; a lot of tents, camp-
stools, tin boxes, white cases, brown bales would be shot down
in the courtyard, and the air of mystery would deepen a little over
the muddle of the station. Five such instalments came, with their
absurd air of disorderly flight with the loot of innumerable outfit
shops and provision stores, that, one would think, they were lugging, after a raid, into the wilderness for equitable division. It was
an inextricable mess of things decent in themselves but that human folly made look like the spoils of thieving.

"This devoted band called itself the Eldorado Exploring Expedition, and I believe they were sworn to secrecy. Their talk, however, was the talk of sordid buccaneers: it was reckless without
hardihood, greedy without audacity, and cruel without courage;
there was not an atom of foresight or of serious intention in the
whole batch of them, and they did not seem aware these things
are wanted for the work of the world. To tear treasure out of
the bowels of the land was their desire, with no more moral purpose at the back of it than there is in burglars breaking into a safe.
Who paid the expenses of the noble enterprise I don't know; but
the uncle of our manager was leader of that lot.

"In exterior he resembled a butcher in a poor neighbourhood,
and his eyes had a look of sleepy cunning. He carried his fat
paunch with ostentation on his short legs, and during the time his
gang infested the station spoke to no one but his nephew. You
could see these two roaming about all day long with their heads
close together in an everlasting confab.

"I had given up worrying myself about the rivets. One's capacity for that kind of folly is more limited than you would suppose.
I said Hang!—and let things slide. I had plenty of time for meditation, and now and then I would give some thought to Kurtz. I
wasn't very interested in him. No. Still, I was curious to see
whether this man, who had come out equipped with moral ideas
of some sort, would climb to the top after all, and how he would
set about his work when there."

# II

"One evening as I was lying flat on the deck of my steamboat, I heard voices approaching—and there were the nephew and the uncle strolling along the bank. I laid my head on my arm again, and had nearly lost myself in a doze, when somebody said in my ear, as it were: 'I am as harmless as a little child, but I don't like to be dictated to. Am I the manager—or am I not? I was ordered to send him there. It's incredible.' . . . I became aware that the two were standing on the shore alongside the forepart of the steamboat, just below my head. I did not move; it did not occur to me to move: I was sleepy. 'It *is* unpleasant,' grunted the uncle. 'He has asked the Administration to be sent there,' said the other, 'with the idea of showing what he could do; and I was instructed accordingly. Look at the influence that man must have. Is it not frightful?' They both agreed it was frightful, then made several bizarre remarks: 'Make rain and fine weather—one man—the Council—by the nose'—bits of absurd sentences that got the better of my drowsiness, so that I had pretty near the whole of my wits about me when the uncle said, 'The climate may do away with this difficulty for you. Is he alone there?' 'Yes,' answered the manager; 'he sent his assistant down the river with a note to me in these terms: "Clear this poor devil out of the country, and don't bother sending more of that sort. I had rather be alone than have the kind of men you can dispose of with me." It was more than a year ago. Can you imagine such impudence!' 'Anything since then?' asked the other, hoarsely. 'Ivory,' jerked out the nephew; 'lots of it—prime sort—lots—most annoying, from him.' 'And with that?' questioned the heavy rumble. 'Invoice,' was the reply fired out, so to speak. Then silence. They had been talking about Kurtz.

"I was broad awake by this time, but, lying perfectly at ease, remained still, having no inducement to change my position. 'How did that ivory come all this way?' growled the elder man, who seemed very vexed. The other explained that it had come with a fleet of canoes in charge of an English half-caste clerk Kurtz had with him; that Kurtz had apparently intended to return himself, the station being by that time bare of goods and stores, but after coming three hundred miles, had suddenly decided to go back, which he started to do alone in a small dug-out with four paddlers, leaving the half-caste to continue down the river with the ivory. The two fellows there seemed astounded at anybody attempting such a thing. They were at a loss for an adequate motive. As to me, I seemed to see Kurtz for the first time. It was a distinct glimpse: the dug-out, four paddling savages, and the lone white man turning his back suddenly on the headquarters, on relief, on thoughts of home—perhaps; setting his face towards the depths of the wilderness, towards his empty and desolate station. I did not know the motive. Perhaps he was just simply a fine fellow who stuck to his work for its own sake. His name, you understand, had not been pronounced once. He was 'that man.' The half-caste, who, as far as I could see, had conducted a difficult trip with great prudence and pluck, was invariably alluded to as 'that scoundrel.' The 'scoundrel' had reported that the 'man' had been very ill—had recovered imperfectly. . . . The two below me moved away then a few paces, and strolled back and forth at some little distance. I heard: 'Military post—doctor—two hundred miles—quite alone now—unavoidable delays—nine months—no news—strange rumours.' They approached again, just as the manager was saying, 'No one, as far as I know, unless a species of wandering trader—a pestilential fellow, snapping ivory from the natives.' Who was it they were talking about now? I gathered in snatches that this was some man supposed to be in Kurtz's district, and of whom the manager did not approve. 'We will not be free from unfair competition till one of these fellows is hanged for an example,' he said. 'Certainly,' grunted the other; 'get him hanged! Why not? Anything—anything can be done in this country. That's what I say; nobody here, you understand, *here*, can endanger your position. And why? You stand the climate—you outlast them all. The danger is in Europe; but there before I left I took

care to—' They moved off and whispered, then their voices rose
again. 'The extraordinary series of delays is not my fault. I did my
possible.' The fat man sighed, 'Very sad.' 'And the pestiferous
absurdity of his talk,' continued the other; 'he bothered me
enough when he was here. "Each station should be like a beacon
on the road towards better things, a centre for trade of course, but
also for humanising, improving, instructing." Conceive you—that
ass! And he wants to be manager! No, it's—' Here he got choked
by excessive indignation, and I lifted my head the least bit. I was
surprised to see how near they were—right under me. I could have
spat upon their hats. They were looking on the ground, absorbed
in thought. The manager was switching his leg with a slender
twig: his sagacious relative lifted his head. 'You have been well
since you came out this time?' he asked. The other gave a start.
'Who? I? Oh! Like a charm—like a charm. But the rest—oh, my
goodness! All sick. They die so quick, too, that I haven't the time
to send them out of the country—it's incredible!' 'H'm. Just so,'
grunted the uncle. 'Ah! my boy, trust to this—I say, trust to this.'
I saw him extend his short flipper of an arm for a gesture that
took in the forest, the creek, the mud, the river[1]—seemed to
beckon with a dishonouring flourish before the sunlit face of the
land a treacherous appeal to the lurking death, to the hidden evil,
to the profound darkness of its heart. It was so startling that I
leaped to my feet and looked back at the edge of the forest, as
though I had expected an answer of some sort to that black dis-
play of confidence. You know the foolish notions that come to one
sometimes. The high stillness confronted these two figures with
its ominous patience, waiting for the passing away of a fantastic
invasion.

"They swore aloud together—out of sheer fright, I believe—
then pretending not to know anything of my existence, turned
back to the station. The sun was low; and leaning forward side by
side, they seemed to be tugging painfully uphill their two ridicu-
lous shadows of unequal length, that trailed behind them slowly
over the tall grass without bending a single blade.

"In a few days the Eldorado Expedition went into the patient
wilderness, that closed upon it as the sea closes over a diver. Long
afterwards the news came that all the donkeys were dead. I know
nothing as to the fate of the less valuable animals. They, no doubt,

like the rest of us, found what they deserved. I did not inquire. I was then rather excited at the prospect of meeting Kurtz very soon. When I say very soon I mean it comparatively. It was just two months from the day we left the creek when we came to the bank below Kurtz's station.

"Going up that river was like travelling back to the earliest beginnings of the world, when vegetation rioted on the earth and the big trees were kings. An empty stream, a great silence, an impenetrable forest. The air was warm, thick, heavy, sluggish. There was no joy in the brilliance of sunshine. The long stretches of the waterway ran on, deserted, into the gloom of overshadowed distances. On silvery sandbanks hippos and alligators sunned themselves side by side. The broadening waters flowed through a mob of wooded islands; you lost your way on that river as you would in a desert, and butted all day long against shoals, trying to find the channel, till you thought yourself bewitched and cut off for ever from everything you had known once— somewhere—far away—in another existence perhaps. There were moments when one's past came back to one, as it will sometimes when you have not a moment to spare to yourself; but it came in the shape of an unrestful and noisy dream, remembered with wonder amongst the overwhelming realities of this strange world of plants, and water, and silence. And this stillness of life did not in the least resemble a peace. It was the stillness of an implacable force brooding over an inscrutable intention. It looked at you with a vengeful aspect. I got used to it afterwards; I did not see it any more; I had no time. I had to keep guessing at the channel; I had to discern, mostly by inspiration, the signs of hidden banks; I watched for sunken stones; I was learning to clap my teeth smartly before my heart flew out, when I shaved by a fluke some infernal sly old snag that would have ripped the life out of the tin-pot steamboat and drowned all the pilgrims; I had to keep a lookout for the signs of dead wood we could cut up in the night for next day's steaming. When you have to attend to things of that sort, to the mere incidents of the surface, the reality—the reality, I tell you—fades. The inner truth is hidden—luckily, luckily. But I felt it all the same; I felt often its mysterious stillness watching me at my monkey tricks, just as it watches you fellows performing on your respective tight-ropes for—what is it? half-a-crown a tumble—"

"Try to be civil, Marlow," growled a voice, and I knew there was at least one listener awake besides myself.

"I beg your pardon. I forgot the heartache which makes up the rest of the price. And indeed what does the price matter, if the trick be well done? You do your tricks very well. And I didn't do badly either, since I managed not to sink that steamboat on my first trip. It's a wonder to me yet. Imagine a blindfolded man set to drive a van over a bad road. I sweated and shivered over that business considerably, I can tell you. After all, for a seaman, to scrape the bottom of the thing that's supposed to float all the time under his care is the unpardonable sin. No one may know of it, but you never forget the thump—eh? A blow on the very heart. You remember it, you dream of it, you wake up at night and think of it—years after—and go hot and cold all over. I don't pretend to say that steamboat floated all the time. More than once she had to wade for a bit, with twenty cannibals splashing around and pushing. We had enlisted some of these chaps on the way for a crew. Fine fellows—cannibals—in their place. They were men one could work with, and I am grateful to them.[2] And, after all, they did not eat each other before my face: they had brought along a provision of hippo-meat which went rotten, and made the mystery of the wilderness stink in my nostrils. Phoo! I can sniff it now. I had the manager on board and three or four pilgrims with their staves—all complete. Sometimes we came upon a station close by the bank, clinging to the skirts of the Unknown, and the white men rushing out of a tumble-down hovel, with great gestures of joy and surprise and welcome, seemed very strange—had the appearance of being held there captive by a spell. The word 'ivory' would ring in the air for a while—and on we went again into the silence, along empty reaches, round the still bends, between the high walls of our winding way, reverberating in hollow claps the ponderous beat of the stern-wheel. Trees, trees, millions of trees, massive, immense, running up high; and at their foot, hugging the bank against the stream, crept the little begrimed steamboat, like a sluggish beetle crawling on the floor of a lofty portico. It made you feel very small, very lost, and yet it was not altogether depressing that feeling. After all, if you were small, the grimy beetle crawled on—which was just what you wanted it to do. Where the pilgrims imagined it crawled to I don't know. To some place where they expected to get something, I bet! For me it crawled towards Kurtz—exclusively; but when the steam-pipes started leaking we crawled very slow. The reaches opened before us and closed behind, as if the forest had stepped leisurely across the water to bar the way for our return. We penetrated deeper and deeper into the heart of darkness. It was very quiet there. At night sometimes the roll of drums behind the curtain of trees would run up the river and remain sustained faintly, as if hovering in the air high over our heads, till the first break of day. Whether this meant war, peace, or prayer we could not tell. The dawns were heralded by the descent of a chill stillness; the woodcutters slept, their fires burned low; the snapping of a twig would make you start. We were wanderers on a prehistoric earth, on an earth that wore the aspect of an unknown planet. We could have fancied ourselves the first of men taking possession of an accursed inheritance, to be subdued at the cost of profound anguish and of excessive toil. But suddenly, as we struggled round a bend, there would be a glimpse of rush walls, of peaked grass-roofs, a burst of yells, a whirl of black limbs, a mass of hands clapping, of feet stamping, of bodies swaying, of eyes rolling, under the droop of heavy and motionless foliage. The steamer toiled along slowly on the edge of a black and incomprehensible frenzy. The prehistoric man was cursing us, praying to us, welcoming us—who could tell? We were cut off from the comprehension of our surroundings; we glided past like phantoms, wondering and secretly appalled, as sane men would be before an enthusiastic outbreak in a madhouse. We could not understand, because we were too far and could not remember, because we were travelling in the night of first ages, of those ages that are gone, leaving hardly a sign—and no memories.[3]

"The earth seemed unearthly. We are accustomed to look upon the shackled form of a conquered monster, but there—there you could look at a thing monstrous and free. It was unearthly, and the men were—No, they were not inhuman. Well, you know, that was the worst of it—this suspicion of their not being inhuman. It would come slowly to one. They howled, and leaped, and spun, and made horrid faces; but what thrilled you was just the thought of their humanity—like yours—the thought of your remote kinship with this wild and passionate uproar. Ugly. Yes, it was ugly enough; but if you were man enough you would admit to yourself that there was in you just the faintest trace of a response to the terrible frankness of that noise, a dim suspicion of there being a meaning in it which you—you so remote from the night of first ages—could comprehend. And why not? The mind of man is capable of anything—because everything is in it, all the past as well as all the future. What was there after all? Joy, fear, sorrow, devotion, valour, rage—who can tell?—but truth—truth stripped of its cloak of time. Let the fool gape and shudder—the man knows, and can look on without a wink. But he must at least be as much of a man as these on the shore. He must meet that truth with his own true stuff—with his own inborn strength. Principles? Principles won't do. Acquisitions, clothes, pretty rags—rags that would fly off at the first good shake. No; you want a deliberate belief. An appeal to me in this fiendish row—is there? Very well; I hear; I admit, but I have a voice too, and for good or evil mine is the speech that cannot be silenced. Of course, a fool, what with sheer fright and fine sentiments, is always safe. Who's that grunting? You wonder I didn't go ashore for a howl and a dance? Well, no—I didn't. Fine sentiments, you say? Fine sentiments, be hanged! I had no time. I had to mess about with white-lead and strips of woollen blanket helping to put bandages on those leaky steam-pipes—I tell you. I had to watch the steering, and circumvent those snags, and get the tin-pot along by hook or by crook. There was surface-truth enough in these things to save a wiser man. And between whiles I had to look after the savage who was fireman. He was an improved specimen; he could fire up a vertical boiler. He was there below me, and, upon my word, to look at him was as edifying as seeing a dog in a parody of breeches and a feather hat, walking on his hind-legs. A few months of training had done for that really fine chap. He squinted at the steam-gauge and at the water-gauge with an evident effort of intrepidity—and he had filed teeth too, the poor devil, and the wool of his pate shaved into queer patterns, and three ornamental scars on each of his cheeks. He ought to have been clapping his hands and stamping his feet on the bank, instead of which he was hard at work, a thrall to strange witchcraft, full of improving knowledge. He was useful because he had been instructed; and what he knew was this—that should the water in that transparent thing disappear, the evil spirit inside the boiler would get angry through the great-

ness of his thirst, and take a terrible vengeance. So he sweated and
fired up and watched the glass fearfully (with an impromptu
charm, made of rags, tied to his arm, and a piece of polished
bone, as big as a watch, stuck flatways through his lower lip),
while the wooded banks slipped past us slowly, the shore noise
was left behind, the interminable miles of silence—and we crept
on, towards Kurtz. But the snags were thick, the water was treacherous and shallow, the boiler seemed indeed to have a sulky devil
in it, and thus neither that fireman nor I had any time to peer into
our creepy thoughts.

"Some fifty miles below the Inner Station we came upon a hut
of reeds, an inclined and melancholy pole, with the unrecognisa-
ble tatters of what had been a flag of some sort flying from it, and
a neatly stacked wood-pile. This was unexpected. We came to the
bank, and on the stack of firewood found a flat piece of board
with some faded pencil-writing on it. When deciphered it said:
'Wood for you. Hurry up. Approach cautiously.' There was a sig-
nature, but it was illegible—not Kurtz—a much longer word.
Hurry up. Where? Up the river? 'Approach cautiously.' We had
not done so. But the warning could not have been meant for the
place where it could be only found after approach. Something was
wrong above. But what—and how much? That was the question.
We commented adversely upon the imbecility of that telegraphic
style. The bush around said nothing, and would not let us look
very far, either. A torn curtain of red twill hung in the doorway
of the hut, and flapped sadly in our faces. The dwelling was dismantled; but we could see a white man had lived there not very
long ago. There remained a rude table—a plank on two posts; a
heap of rubbish reposed in a dark corner, and by the door I picked
up a book. It had lost its covers, and the pages had been thumbed
into a state of extremely dirty softness; but the back had been
lovingly stitched afresh with white cotton thread, which looked
clean yet. It was an extraordinary find. Its title was, 'An Inquiry
into some Points of Seamanship,' by a man Towzer, Towson—
some such name—Master in his Majesty's Navy. The matter
looked dreary reading enough, with illustrative diagrams and
repulsive tables of figures, and the copy was sixty years old. I
handled this amazing antiquity with the greatest possible tender-
ness, lest it should dissolve in my hands. Within, Towson or Tow-

zer was inquiring earnestly into the breaking strain of ships'
chains and tackle, and other such matters. Not a very enthralling
book; but at the first glance you could see there a singleness of
intention, an honest concern for the right way of going to work,
which made these humble pages, thought out so many years ago,
luminous with another than a professional light.[4] The simple old
sailor, with his talk of chains and purchases, made me forget the
jungle and the pilgrims in a delicious sensation of having come
upon something unmistakably real. Such a book being there was
wonderful enough; but still more astounding were the notes pen-
cilled in the margin, and plainly referring to the text. I couldn't
believe my eyes! They were in cipher! Yes, it looked like cipher.
Fancy a man lugging with him a book of that description into this
nowhere and studying it—and making notes—in cipher at that! It
was an extravagant mystery.

"I had been dimly aware for some time of a worrying noise, and
when I lifted my eyes I saw the wood-pile was gone, and the manager, aided by all the pilgrims, was shouting at me from the river-
side. I slipped the book into my pocket. I assure you to leave off
reading was like tearing myself away from the shelter of an old
and solid friendship.

"I started the lame engine ahead. 'It must be this miserable
trader—this intruder,' exclaimed the manager, looking back ma-
levolently at the place we had left. 'He must be English,' I said. 'It
will not save him from getting into trouble if he is not careful,'
muttered the manager darkly. I observed with assumed innocence
that no man was safe from trouble in this world.

"The current was more rapid now, the steamer seemed at her
last gasp, the stern-wheel flopped languidly, and I caught myself
listening on tiptoe for the next beat of the float, for in sober truth
I expected the wretched thing to give up every moment. It was like
watching the last flickers of a life. But still we crawled. Sometimes
I would pick out a tree a little way ahead to measure our progress
towards Kurtz by, but I lost it invariably before we got abreast. To
keep the eyes so long on one thing was too much for human patience. The manager displayed a beautiful resignation. I fretted
and fumed and took to arguing with myself whether or no I would
talk openly with Kurtz; but before I could come to any conclusion
it occurred to me that my speech or my silence, indeed any action

of mine, would be a mere futility. What did it matter what any one knew or ignored? What did it matter who was manager? One gets sometimes such a flash of insight. The essentials of this affair lay deep under the surface, beyond my reach, and beyond my power of meddling.

"Towards the evening of the second day we judged ourselves about eight miles from Kurtz's station. I wanted to push on; but the manager looked grave, and told me the navigation up there was so dangerous that it would be advisable, the sun being very low already, to wait where we were till next morning. Moreover, he pointed out that if the warning to approach cautiously were to be followed, we must approach in daylight—not at dusk, or in the dark. This was sensible enough. Eight miles meant nearly three hours' steaming for us, and I could also see suspicious ripples at the upper end of the reach. Nevertheless, I was annoyed beyond expression at the delay, and most unreasonably too, since one night more could not matter much after so many months. As we had plenty of wood, and caution was the word, I brought up in the middle of the stream. The reach was narrow, straight, with high sides like a railway cutting. The dusk came gliding into it long before the sun had set. The current ran smooth and swift, but a dumb immobility sat on the banks. The living trees, lashed together by the creepers and every living bush of the undergrowth, might have been changed into stone, even to the slenderest twig, to the lightest leaf. It was not sleep—it seemed unnatural, like a state of trance. Not the faintest sound of any kind could be heard. You looked on amazed, and began to suspect yourself of being deaf—then the night came suddenly, and struck you blind as well. About three in the morning some large fish leaped, and the loud splash made me jump as though a gun had been fired. When the sun rose there was a white fog, very warm and clammy, and more blinding than the night. It did not shift or drive; it was just there, standing all round you like something solid. At eight or nine, perhaps, it lifted as a shutter lifts. We had a glimpse of the towering multitude of trees, of the immense matted jungle, with the blazing little ball of the sun hanging over it—all perfectly still—and then the white shutter came down again, smoothly, as if sliding in greased grooves. I ordered the chain, which we had begun to heave in, to be paid out again. Before it stopped running

with a muffled rattle, a cry, a very loud cry, as of infinite desolation, soared slowly in the opaque air. It ceased. A complaining
clamour, modulated in savage discords, filled our ears. The sheer
unexpectedness of it made my hair stir under my cap. I don't
know how it struck the others: to me it seemed as though the mist
itself had screamed, so suddenly, and apparently from all sides at
once, did this tumultuous and mournful uproar arise. It culmi-
nated in a hurried outbreak of almost intolerably excessive shriek-
ing, which stopped short, leaving us stiffened in a variety of silly
attitudes, and obstinately listening to the nearly as appalling and
excessive silence. 'Good God! What is the meaning—?' stammered
at my elbow one of the pilgrims—a little fat man, with sandy hair
and red whiskers, who wore side-spring boots, and pink pyjamas
tucked into his socks. Two others remained open-mouthed a
whole minute, then dashed into the little cabin, to rush out incon-
tinently and stand darting scared glances, with Winchesters at
'ready' in their hands. What we could see was just the steamer
we were on, her outlines blurred as though she had been on the
point of dissolving, and a misty strip of water, perhaps two feet
broad, around her—and that was all. The rest of the world was
nowhere, as far as our eyes and ears were concerned. Just nowhere. Gone, disappeared; swept off without leaving a whisper or
a shadow behind.

"I went forward, and ordered the chain to be hauled in short,
so as to be ready to trip the anchor and move the steamboat at
once if necessary. 'Will they attack?' whispered an awed voice.
'We will be all butchered in this fog,' murmured another. The
faces twitched with the strain, the hands trembled slightly, the
eyes forgot to wink. It was very curious to see the contrast of
expressions of the white men and of the black fellows of our crew,
who were as much strangers to that part of the river as we, though
their homes were only eight hundred miles away. The whites, of
course greatly discomposed, had besides a curious look of being
painfully shocked by such an outrageous row. The others had an
alert, naturally interested expression; but their faces were essentially quiet, even those of the one or two who grinned as they
hauled at the chain. Several exchanged short, grunting phrases,
which seemed to settle the matter to their satisfaction. Their headman, a young, broad-chested black, severely draped in dark-blue

fringed cloths, with fierce nostrils and his hair all done up artfully in oily ringlets, stood near me. 'Aha!' I said nodding, just for good fellowship's sake. 'Catch 'im,' he snapped, with a bloodshot widening of his eyes and a flash of sharp teeth—'catch 'im. Give 'im to us.' 'To you, eh?' I asked; 'what would you do with them?' 'Eat 'im!' he said, curtly, and, leaning his elbow on the rail, looked out into the fog in a dignified and profoundly pensive attitude. I would no doubt have been properly horrified, had it not occurred to me that he and his chaps must be very hungry: that they must have been growing increasingly hungry for at least this month past. They had been engaged for six months (I don't think a single one of them had any clear idea of time, as we at the end of countless ages have. They still belonged to the beginnings of time—had no inherited experience to teach them as it were), and of course, as long as there was a piece of paper written over in accordance with some farcical law or other made down the river, it didn't enter anybody's head to trouble how they would live. Certainly they had brought with them some rotten hippo-meat, which couldn't have lasted very long, anyway, even if the pilgrims hadn't, in the midst of a shocking hullabaloo, thrown a considerable quantity of it overboard. It looked like a high-handed proceeding; but it was really a case of legitimate self-defence. You can't breathe dead hippo waking, sleeping, and eating, and at the same time keep your precarious grip on existence. Besides that, they had given them every week three pieces of brass wire, each about nine inches long; and the theory was they were to buy their provisions with that currency in river-side villages. You can see how *that* worked. There were either no villages, or the people were hostile, or the director, who like the rest of us fed out of tins, with an occasional old he-goat thrown in, didn't want to stop the steamer for some more or less recondite reason. So, unless they swallowed the wire itself, or made loops of it to snare the fish with, I don't see what good their extravagant salary could be to them.[5] I must say it was paid with a regularity worthy of a large and honourable trading company. For the rest, the only thing to eat—though it didn't look eatable in the least—I saw in their possession was a few lumps of some stuff like half-cooked cold dough, of a dirty lavender colour, they kept wrapped in leaves, and now and then swallowed a piece of, but so small that it seemed done more for the looks of the thing than for any serious purpose of sustenance. Why in the name of all the gnawing devils of hunger they didn't go for us—they were thirty to five—and have a good tuck in for once, amazes me now when I think of it. They were big powerful men, with not much capacity to weigh the consequences, with courage, with strength, even yet, though their skins were no longer glossy and their muscles no longer hard. And I saw that something restraining, one of those human secrets that baffle probability, had come into play there. I looked at them with a swift quickening of interest—not because it occurred to me I might be eaten by them before very long, though I own to you that just then I perceived—in a new light, as it were—how unwholesome the pilgrims looked, and I hoped, yes, I positively hoped, that my aspect was not so—what shall I say?—so—unappetising: a touch of fantastic vanity which fitted well with the dream-sensation that pervaded all my days at that time. Perhaps I had a little fever too. One can't live with one's finger everlastingly on one's pulse. I had often a 'little fever,' or a little touch of other things—the playful paw-strokes of the wilderness, the preliminary trifling before the more serious onslaught which came in due course. Yes; I looked at them as you would on any human being, with a curiosity of their impulses, motives, capacities, weaknesses, when brought to the test of an inexorable physical necessity.[6] Restraint! What possible restraint? Was it superstition, disgust, patience, fear—or some kind of primitive honour? No fear can stand up to hunger, no patience can wear it out, disgust simply does not exist where hunger is; and as to superstition, beliefs, and what you may call principles, they are less than chaff in a breeze. Don't you know the devilry of lingering starvation, its exasperating torment, its black thoughts, its sombre and brooding ferocity? Well, I do. It takes a man all his inborn strength to fight hunger properly. It's really easier to face bereavement, dishonour, and the perdition of one's soul—than this kind of prolonged hunger. Sad, but true. And these chaps too had no earthly reason for any kind of scruple. Restraint! I would just as soon have expected restraint from a hyena prowling amongst the corpses of a battlefield. But there was the fact facing me—the fact dazzling, to be seen, like the foam on the depths of the sea, like a ripple on an unfathomable enigma, a mystery greater—when I thought of it—than the curious, inexplicable note of desperate grief in this savage clamour that had swept by us on the river-bank, behind the blind whiteness of a fog.

"Two pilgrims were quarrelling in hurried whispers as to which bank. 'Left.' 'No, no; how can you? Right, right, of course.' 'It is serious, very serious,' said the manager's voice behind me; 'I would be desolated if anything should happen to Mr Kurtz before we came up.' I looked at him, and had not the slightest doubt he was sincere. He was just the kind of man who would wish to preserve appearances. That was his restraint. But when he muttered something about going on at once, I did not even take the trouble to answer him. I knew, and he knew, that it was impossible. Were we to let go our hold of the bottom, we would be absolutely in the air—in space. We wouldn't be able to tell where we were going to—whether up or down stream, or across—till we fetched against one bank or the other—and then we wouldn't know at first which it was. Of course I made no move. I had no mind for a smash-up. You couldn't imagine a more deadly place for a shipwreck. Whether drowned at once or not, we were sure to perish speedily in one way or another. 'I authorise you to take all the risks,' he said, after a short silence. 'I refuse to take any,' I said shortly; which was just the answer he expected, though its tone might have surprised him. 'Well, I must defer to your judgment. You are captain,' he said, with marked civility. I turned my shoulder to him in sign of my appreciation, and looked into the fog. How long would it last? It was the most hopeless look-out. The approach to this Kurtz grubbing for ivory in the wretched bush was beset by as many dangers as though he had been an enchanted princess sleeping in a fabulous castle.[7] 'Will they attack, do you think?' asked the manager, in a confidential tone.

"I did not think they would attack, for several obvious reasons. The thick fog was one. If they left the bank in their canoes they would get lost in it, as we would be if we attempted to move. Still, I had also judged the jungle of both banks quite impenetrable— and yet eyes were in it, eyes that had seen us. The river-side bushes were certainly very thick; but the undergrowth behind was evidently penetrable. However, during the short lift I had seen no canoes anywhere in the reach—certainly not abreast of the steamer. But what made the idea of attack inconceivable to me was the nature of the noise—of the cries we had heard. They had not the fierce character boding of immediate hostile intention. Unexpected, wild, and violent as they had been, they had given me an irresistible impression of sorrow. The glimpse of the steamboat had for some reason filled those savages with unrestrained grief. The danger, if any, I expounded, was from our proximity to a great human passion let loose. Even extreme grief may ultimately vent itself in violence—but more generally takes the form of apathy. . . .

"You should have seen the pilgrims stare! They had no heart to grin, or even to revile me; but I believe they thought me gone mad—with fright, maybe. I delivered a regular lecture. My dear boys, it was no good bothering. Keep a look-out? Well, you may guess I watched the fog for the signs of lifting as a cat watches a mouse; but for anything else our eyes were of no more use to us than if we had been buried miles deep in a heap of cotton-wool. It felt like it too—choking, warm, stifling. Besides, all I said, though it sounded extravagant, was absolutely true to fact. What we afterwards alluded to as an attack was really an attempt at repulse. The action was very far from being aggressive—it was not even defensive, in the usual sense: it was undertaken under the stress of desperation, and in its essence was purely protective.

"It developed itself, I should say, two hours after the fog lifted, and its commencement was at a spot, roughly speaking, about a mile and a half below Kurtz's station. We had just floundered and flopped round a bend, when I saw an islet, a mere grassy hummock of bright green, in the middle of the stream. It was the only thing of the kind; but as we opened the reach more, I perceived it was the head of a long sandbank, or rather of a chain of shallow patches stretching down the middle of the river. They were discoloured, just awash, and the whole lot was seen just under the water, exactly as a man's backbone is seen running down the middle of his back under the skin. Now, as far as I did see, I could go to the right or to the left of this. I didn't know either channel, of course. The banks looked pretty well alike, the depth appeared the same; but as I had been informed the station was on the west side, I naturally headed for the western passage.

"No sooner had we fairly entered it than I became aware it was much narrower than I had supposed. To the left of us there was the long uninterrupted shoal, and to the right a high, steep bank heavily overgrown with bushes. Above the bush the trees stood in serried ranks. The twigs overhung the current thickly, and from distance to distance a large limb of some tree projected rigidly over the stream. It was then well on in the afternoon, the face of the forest was gloomy, and a broad strip of shadow had already fallen on the water. In this shadow we steamed up—very slowly, as you may imagine. I sheered her well inshore—the water being deepest near the bank, as the sounding-pole informed me.

"One of my hungry and forbearing friends was sounding in the bows just below me. This steamboat was exactly like a decked scow. On the deck there were two little teak-wood houses, with doors and windows. The boiler was in the fore-end, and the machinery right astern. Over the whole there was a light roof, supported on stanchions. The funnel projected through that roof, and just in front of the funnel a small cabin built of light planks served for a pilot-house. It contained a couch, two camp-stools, a loaded Martini-Henry leaning in one corner, a tiny table, and the steering-wheel. It had a wide door in front and a broad shutter at each side. All these were always thrown open, of course. I spent my days perched up there on the extreme fore-end of that roof, before the door. At night I slept, or tried to, on the couch. An athletic black belonging to some coast tribe, and educated by my poor predecessor, was the helmsman. He sported a pair of brass earrings, wore a blue cloth wrapper from the waist to the ankles, and thought all the world of himself. He was the most unstable kind of fool I had ever seen. He steered with no end of a swagger while you were by; but if he lost sight of you, he became instantly the prey of an abject funk, and would let that cripple of a steamboat get the upper hand of him in a minute.

"I was looking down at the sounding-pole, and feeling much annoyed to see at each try a little more of it stick out of that river, when I saw my poleman give up the business suddenly, and stretch himself flat on the deck, without even taking the trouble to haul his pole in. He kept hold on it though, and it trailed in the water. At the same time the fireman, whom I could also see below me, sat down abruptly before his furnace and ducked his head. I was amazed. Then I had to look at the river mighty quick, because there was a snag in the fairway. Sticks, little sticks, were flying

about—thick: they were whizzing before my nose, dropping below me, striking behind me against my pilot-house. All this time
the river, the shore, the woods, were very quiet—perfectly quiet.
I could only hear the heavy splashy thump of the stern-wheel and
the patter of these things. We cleared the snag clumsily. Arrows,
by Jove![8] We were being shot at! I stepped in quickly to close the
shutter on the land-side. That fool-helmsman, his hands on the
spokes, was lifting his knees high, stamping his feet, champing his
mouth, like a reined-in horse. Confound him! And we were stag-
gering within ten feet of the bank. I had to lean right out to swing
the heavy shutter, and I saw a face amongst the leaves on the level
with my own, looking at me very fierce and steady; and then suddenly, as though a veil had been removed from my eyes, I made
out, deep in the tangled gloom, naked breasts, arms, legs, glaring eyes—the bush was swarming with human limbs in movement, glistening, of bronze colour. The twigs shook, swayed, and
rustled, the arrows flew out of them, and then the shutter came
to. 'Steer her straight,' I said to the helmsman. He held his head
rigid, face forward; but his eyes rolled, he kept on lifting and setting down his feet gently, his mouth foamed a little. 'Keep quiet!'
I said in a fury. I might just as well have ordered a tree not to sway
in the wind. I darted out. Below me there was a great scuffle of
feet on the iron deck; confused exclamations; a voice screamed,
'Can you turn back?' I caught sight of a V-shaped ripple on the
water ahead. What? Another snag! A fusillade burst out under my
feet. The pilgrims had opened fire with their Winchesters, and
were simply squirting lead into that bush. A deuce of a lot of
smoke came up and drove slowly forward. I swore at it. Now I
couldn't see the ripple or the snag either.[9] I stood in the doorway,
peering, and the arrows came in swarms. They might have been
poisoned, but they looked as though they wouldn't kill a cat. The
bush began to howl. Our wood-cutters raised a warlike whoop;
the report of a rifle just at my back deafened me. I glanced over
my shoulder, and the pilot-house was yet full of noise and smoke
when I made a dash at the wheel. The fool-nigger had dropped
everything, to throw the shutter open and let off that Martini-
Henry. He stood before the wide opening, glaring, and I yelled at
him to come back, while I straightened the sudden twist out of
that steamboat. There was no room to turn even if I had wanted

to, the snag was somewhere very near ahead in that confounded smoke, there was no time to lose, so I just crowded her into the bank—right into the bank, where I knew the water was deep.

"We tore slowly along the overhanging bushes in a whirl of broken twigs and flying leaves. The fusillade below stopped short, as I had foreseen it would when the squirts got empty. I threw my head back to a glinting whizz that traversed the pilot-house, in at one shutter-hole and out at the other. Looking past that mad helmsman, who was shaking the empty rifle and yelling at the shore, I saw vague forms of men running bent double, leaping, gliding, distinct, incomplete, evanescent. Something big appeared in the air before the shutter, the rifle went overboard, and the man stepped back swiftly, looked at me over his shoulder in an extraordinary, profound, familiar manner, and fell upon my feet. The side of his head hit the wheel twice, and the end of what appeared a long cane clattered round and knocked over a little camp-stool. It looked as though after wrenching that thing from somebody ashore he had lost his balance in the effort. The thin smoke had blown away, we were clear of the snag, and looking ahead I could see that in another hundred yards or so I would be free to sheer off, away from the bank; but my feet felt so very warm and wet that I had to look down. The man had rolled on his back and stared straight up at me; both his hands clutched that cane. It was the shaft of a spear that, either thrown or lounged through the opening, had caught him in the side just below the ribs; the blade had gone in out of sight, after making a frightful gash; my shoes were full; a pool of blood lay very still, gleaming dark-red under the wheel; his eyes shone with an amazing lustre. The fusillade burst out again. He looked at me anxiously, gripping the spear like something precious, with an air of being afraid I would try to take it away from him. I had to make an effort to free my eyes from his gaze and attend to the steering. With one hand I felt above my head for the line of the steam-whistle, and jerked out screech after screech hurriedly. The tumult of angry and warlike yells was checked instantly, and then from the depths of the woods went out such a tremulous and prolonged wail of mournful fear and utter despair as may be imagined to follow the flight of the last hope from the earth. There was a great commotion in the bush; the shower of arrows stopped, a few dropping shots rang out sharply—then silence, in which the languid beat of the stern-wheel came plainly to my ears. I put the helm hard a-starboard at the moment when the pilgrim in pink pyjamas, very hot and agitated, appeared in the doorway. 'The manager sends me—' he began in an official tone, and stopped short. 'Good God!' he said, glaring at the wounded man.

"We two whites stood over him, and his lustrous and inquiring glance enveloped us both. I declare it looked as though he would presently put to us some question in an understandable language; but he died without uttering a sound, without moving a limb, without twitching a muscle. Only in the very last moment, as though in response to some sign we could not see, to some whisper we could not hear, he frowned heavily, and that frown gave to his black death-mask an inconceivably sombre, brooding, and menacing expression. The lustre of inquiring glance faded swiftly into vacant glassiness. 'Can you steer?' I asked the agent eagerly. He looked very dubious; but I made a grab at his arm, and he understood at once I meant him to steer whether or no. To tell you the truth, I was morbidly anxious to change my shoes and socks. 'He is dead,' murmured the fellow, immensely impressed. 'No doubt about it,' said I, tugging like mad at the shoe-laces. 'And, by the way, I suppose Mr Kurtz is dead as well by this time.'

"For the moment that was the dominant thought. There was a sense of extreme disappointment, as though I had found out I had been striving after something altogether without a substance. I couldn't have been more disgusted if I had travelled all this way for the sole purpose of talking with Mr Kurtz. Talking with . . . I flung one shoe overboard, and became aware that that was exactly what I had been looking forward to—a talk with Kurtz. I made the strange discovery that I had never imagined him as doing, you know, but as discoursing. I didn't say to myself, 'Now I will never see him,' or 'Now I will never shake him by the hand,' but, 'Now I will never hear him.' The man presented himself as a voice. Not of course that I did not connect him with some sort of action. Hadn't I been told in all the tones of jealousy and admiration that he had collected, bartered, swindled, or stolen more ivory than all the other agents together. That was not the point. The point was in his being a gifted creature, and that of all his gifts the one that stood out pre-eminently, that carried with it a sense of real presence, was his ability to talk, his words—the gift of expression, the bewildering, the illuminating, the most exalted and the most contemptible, the pulsating stream of light, or the deceitful flow from the heart of an impenetrable darkness.

"The other shoe went flying unto the devil-god of that river. I thought, By Jove! it's all over. We are too late; he has vanished—the gift has vanished, by means of some spear, arrow, or club. I will never hear that chap speak after all—and my sorrow had a startling extravagance of emotion, even such as I had noticed in the howling sorrow of these savages in the bush. I couldn't have felt more of lonely desolation somehow, had I been robbed of a belief or had missed my destiny in life. . . . Why do you sigh in this beastly way, somebody? Absurd? Well, absurd. Good Lord! mustn't a man ever—Here, give me some tobacco." . . .

There was a pause of profound stillness, then a match flared, and Marlow's lean face appeared—worn, hollow, with downward folds and dropped eyelids, with an aspect of concentrated attention; and as he took vigorous draws at his pipe, it seemed to retreat and advance out of the night in the regular flicker of the tiny flame. The match went out.

"Absurd!" he cried. "This is the worst of trying to tell . . . Here you all are, each moored with two good addresses, like a hulk with two anchors, a butcher round one corner, a policeman round another, excellent appetites, and temperature normal—you hear—normal from year's end to year's end. And you say, Absurd! Absurd be—exploded! Absurd! My dear boys, what can you expect from a man who out of sheer nervousness had just flung overboard a pair of new shoes. Now I think of it, it is amazing I did not shed tears. I am, upon the whole, proud of my fortitude. I was cut to the quick at the idea of having lost the inestimable privilege of listening to the gifted Kurtz. Of course I was wrong. The privilege was waiting for me. Oh yes, I heard more than enough. And I was right, too. A voice. He was very little more than a voice. And I heard—him—it—this voice—other voices—all of them were so little more than voices—and the memory of that time itself lingers around me, impalpable, like a dying vibration of one immense jabber, silly, atrocious, sordid, savage, or simply mean, without any kind of sense. Voices, voices—even the girl herself—now—"

He was silent for a long time.

"I laid the ghost of his gifts at last with a lie," he began suddenly. "Girl! What? Did I mention a girl? Oh, she is out of it—completely. They—the women I mean—are out of it—should be out of it. We must help them to stay in that beautiful world of their own, lest ours gets worse. Oh, she had to be out of it. You should have heard the disinterred body of Mr Kurtz saying, 'My Intended.' You would have perceived directly then how completely she was out of it. And the lofty frontal bone of Mr Kurtz! They say the hair goes on growing sometimes, but this—ah—specimen, was impressively bald. The wilderness had patted him on the head, and, behold, it was like a ball—an ivory ball; it had caressed him, and—lo!—he had withered; it had taken him, loved him, embraced him, got into his veins, consumed his flesh, and sealed his soul to its own by the inconceivable ceremonies of some devilish initiation. He was its spoiled and pampered favourite. Ivory? I should think so. Heaps of it, stacks of it. The old mud shanty was bursting with it. You would think there was not a single tusk left either above or below ground in the whole country. 'Mostly fossil,' the manager had remarked disparagingly. It was no more fossil than I am; but they call it fossil when it is dug up. It appears these niggers do bury the tusks sometimes—but evidently they couldn't bury this parcel deep enough to save the gifted Mr Kurtz from his fate. We filled the steamboat with it, and had to pile a lot on the deck. Thus he could see and enjoy as long as he could see, because the appreciation of this favour had remained with him to the last. You should have heard him say, 'My ivory.' Oh yes, I heard him. 'My Intended, my ivory, my station, my river, my—' Everything belonged to him. It made me hold my breath in expectation of hearing the wilderness burst into a prodigious peal of laughter that would shake the fixed stars in their places. Everything belonged to him—but that was a trifle. The thing was to know what he belonged to, how many powers of darkness claimed him for their own. That was the reflection that made you creepy all over. It was impossible—it was not good for one either—trying to imagine. He had taken a high seat amongst the devils of the land—I mean literally. You can't understand. How could you?—with solid pavement under your feet, surrounded by kind neighbours ready to cheer you or to fall on you,

stepping delicately between the butcher and the policeman, in the
holy terror of scandal and gallows and lunatic asylums—how can
you imagine what particular region of the first ages a man's un-
trammelled feet may take him into by the way of solitude—utter
solitude without a policeman—by the way of silence—utter silence, where no warning voice of a kind neighbour can be heard
whispering of public opinion? These little things make all the
great difference. When they are gone you must fall back upon
your own innate strength, upon your own capacity for faithful-
ness. Of course you may be too much of a fool to go wrong—too
dull even to know you are being assaulted by the powers of darkness. I take it, no fool ever made a bargain for his soul with the
devil: the fool is too much of a fool, or the devil too much of a
devil—I don't know which. Or you may be such a thunderingly
exalted creature as to be altogether deaf and blind to anything but
heavenly sights and sounds. Then the earth for you is only a
standing place—and whether to be like this is your loss or your
gain I won't pretend to say. But most of us are neither one nor the
other. The earth for us is a place to live in, where we must put up
with sights, with sounds, with smells too, by Jove!—breathe dead
hippo, so to speak, and not be contaminated.[10] And there, don't
you see? your strength comes in, the faith in your ability for the
digging of unostentatious holes to bury the stuff in—your power
of devotion, not to yourself, but to an obscure, back-breaking
business. And that's difficult enough. Mind, I am not trying to
excuse or even explain—I am trying to account to myself for—
for—Mr Kurtz—for the shade of Mr Kurtz. This initiated wraith
from the back of Nowhere honoured me with its amazing confidence before it vanished altogether. This was because it could
speak English to me. The original Kurtz had been educated partly
in England, and—as he was good enough to say himself—his
sympathies were in the right place. His mother was half-English,
his father was half-French. All Europe contributed to the making
of Kurtz; and by and bye I learned that, most appropriately, the
International Society for the Suppression of Savage Customs had
entrusted him with the making of a report, for its future guidance. And he had written it too. I've seen it. I've read it. It was
eloquent, vibrating with eloquence, but too high-strung, I think.
Seventeen pages of close writing he had found time for! But this

must have been before his—let us say—nerves, went wrong, and caused him to preside at certain midnight dances ending with unspeakable rites, which—as far as I reluctantly gathered from what I heard at various times—were offered up to him—do you understand?—to Mr Kurtz himself. But it was a beautiful piece of writing. The opening paragraph, however, in the light of later information, strikes me now as ominous. He began with the argument that we whites, from the point of development we had arrived at, 'must necessarily appear to them [savages] in the nature of supernatural beings—we approach them with the might as of a deity,' and so on, and so on. 'By the simple exercise of our will we can exert a power for good practically unbounded,' etc., etc.[11] From that point he soared and took me with him. The peroration was magnificent, though difficult to remember, you know. It gave me the notion of an exotic Immensity ruled by an august Benevolence. It made me tingle with enthusiasm. This was the unbounded power of eloquence—of words—of burning noble words. There were no practical hints to interrupt the magic current of phrases, unless a kind of note at the foot of the last page, scrawled evidently much later, in an unsteady hand, may be regarded as the exposition of a method. It was very simple, and at the end of that moving appeal to every altruistic sentiment it blazed at you, luminous and terrifying, like a flash of lightning in a serene sky: 'Exterminate all the brutes!' The curious part was that he had apparently forgotten all about that valuable postscriptum, because, later on, when he in a sense came to himself, he repeatedly entreated me to take good care of 'my pamphlet' (he called it), as it was sure to have in the future a good influence upon his career. I had full information about all these things, and, besides, as it turned out, I was to have the care of his memory. I've done enough for it to give me the indisputable right to lay it, if I choose, for an everlasting rest in the dust-bin of progress, amongst all the sweepings and, figuratively speaking, all the dead cats of civilisation. But then, you see, I can't choose. He won't be forgotten. Whatever he was, he was not common. He had the power to charm or frighten rudimentary souls into an aggravated witch-dance in his honour; he could also fill the small souls of the pilgrims with bitter misgivings;[12] he had one devoted friend at least, and he had conquered one soul in the world that was neither rudimentary nor

tainted with self-seeking. No; I can't forget him, though I am not
prepared to affirm the fellow was exactly worth the life we lost in
getting to him. I missed my late helmsman awfully—I missed him
even while his body was still lying in the pilot-house. Perhaps you
will think it passing strange this regret for a savage who was no
more account than a grain of sand in a black Sahara. Well, don't
you see, he had done something, he had steered; for months I had
him at my back—a help—an instrument. It was a kind of partnership. He steered for me—I had to look after him, I worried about
his deficiencies, and thus a subtle bond had been created, of which
I only became aware when it was suddenly broken. And the inti-
mate profundity of that look he gave me when he received his hurt
remains to this day in my memory—like a claim of distant kinship
affirmed in a supreme moment.

"Poor fool! If he had only left that shutter alone. He had no
restraint, no restraint—just like Kurtz—a tree swayed by the
wind. As soon as I had put on a dry pair of slippers, I dragged him
out, after first jerking the spear out of his side, which operation I
confess I performed with my eyes shut tight. His heels leaped together over the little door-step; his shoulders were pressed to my
breast; I hugged him from behind desperately. Oh! he was heavy,
heavy; heavier than any man on earth, I should imagine. Then
without more ado I tipped him overboard. The current snatched
him as though he had been a wisp of grass, and I saw the body
roll over twice before I lost sight of it for ever. All the pilgrims and
the manager were then congregated on the awning-deck about the
pilot-house, chattering at each other like a flock of excited mag-
pies, and there was a scandalised murmur at my heartless promp-
titude. What they wanted to keep that body hanging about for
I can't guess. Embalm it, maybe. But I had also heard another,
and very ominous, murmur on the deck below. My friends the
wood-cutters were likewise scandalised, and with a better show
of reason—though I admit that the reason itself was quite inad-
missible. Oh, quite! I had made up my mind that if my late helmsman was to be eaten, the fishes alone should have him. He had
been a very second-rate helmsman while alive, but now he was
dead he might have become a first-class temptation, and possibly
cause some startling trouble. Besides, I was anxious to take the
wheel, the man in pink pyjamas showing himself a hopeless duffer
at the business.

"This I did directly the simple funeral was over. We were going half-speed, keeping right in the middle of the stream, and I listened to the talk about me. They had given up Kurtz, they had given up the station; Kurtz was dead, and the station had been burnt—and so on—and so on. The red-haired pilgrim was beside himself with the thought that at least this poor Kurtz had been properly revenged. 'Say! We must have made a glorious slaughter of them in the bush. Eh? What do you think? Say?' He positively danced, the bloodthirsty little gingery beggar. And he had nearly fainted when he saw the wounded man! I could not help saying, 'You made a glorious lot of smoke, anyhow.' I had seen, from the way the tops of the bushes rustled and flew, that almost all the shots had gone too high. You can't hit anything unless you take aim and fire from the shoulder; but these chaps fired from the hip with their eyes shut. The retreat, I maintained—and I was right—was caused by the screeching of the steam-whistle. Upon this they forgot Kurtz, and began to howl at me with indignant protests.

"The manager stood by the wheel murmuring confidentially about the necessity of getting well away down the river before dark at all events, when I saw in the distance a clearing on the river-side and the outlines of some sort of building. 'What's this?' I asked. He clapped his hands in wonder. 'The station!' he cried. I edged in at once, still going half-speed.

"Through my glasses I saw the slope of a hill interspersed with rare trees and perfectly free from undergrowth. A long decaying building on the summit was half buried in the high grass; the large holes in the peaked roof gaped black from afar; the jungle and the woods made a background. There was no enclosure or fence of any kind; but there had been one apparently, for near the house half-a-dozen slim posts remained in a row, roughly trimmed, and with their upper ends ornamented with round carved balls. The rails, or whatever there had been between, had disappeared. Of course the forest surrounded all that. The river-bank was clear, and on the water-side I saw a white man under a hat like a cart-wheel beckoning persistently with his whole arm. Examining the edge of the forest above and below, I was almost certain I could see movements—human forms gliding here and there. I steamed past prudently, then stopped the engines and let her drift down. The man on the shore began to shout, urging us to land. 'We have been attacked,' screamed the manager. 'I know—I know. It's all right,' yelled back the other, as cheerful as you please. 'Come along. It's all right. I am glad.'

"His aspect reminded me of something I had seen—something funny I had seen somewhere. As I manoeuvred to get alongside, I was asking myself, 'What does this fellow look like?' Suddenly I got it. He looked like a harlequin. His clothes had been made of some stuff that was brown holland probably, but it was covered with patches all over, with bright patches, blue, red, and yellow— patches on the back, patches on front, patches on elbows, on knees; coloured binding round his jacket, scarlet edging at the bottom of his trousers; and the sunshine made him look extremely gay and wonderfully neat withal, because you could see how beautifully all this patching had been done. A beardless, boyish face, very fair, no features to speak of, nose peeling, little blue eyes, smiles and frowns chasing each other over that open coun- tenance like sunshine and shadow on a wind-swept plain. 'Look out, captain!' he cried; 'there's a snag lodged in here last night.' What! Another snag? I confess I swore shamefully. I had nearly holed my cripple, to finish off that charming trip. The harlequin on the bank turned his little pug nose up to me. 'You English?' he asked, all smiles. 'Are you?' I shouted from the wheel. The smiles vanished, and he shook his head as if sorry for my disappoint- ment. Then he brightened up. 'Never mind!' he cried encourag- ingly. 'Are we in time?' I asked. 'He is up there,' he replied, with a toss of the head up the hill, and becoming gloomy all of a sud- den. His face was like the autumn sky, overcast one moment and bright the next.

"When the manager, escorted by the pilgrims, all of them armed to the teeth, had gone to the house, this chap came on board. 'I say, I don't like this. These natives are in the bush,' I said. He as- sured me earnestly it was all right. 'They are simple people,' he added; 'well, I am glad you came. It took me all my time to keep them off.' 'But you said it was all right,' I cried. 'Oh, they meant no harm,' he said; and as I stared he corrected himself, 'Not ex- actly.' Then vivaciously, 'My faith, your pilot-house wants a clean up!' In the next breath he advised me to keep enough steam on the boiler to blow the whistle in case of any trouble. 'One good screech will do more for you than all your rifles. They are simple people,' he repeated. He rattled away at such a rate he quite over-

whelmed me. He seemed to be trying to make up for lots of silence, and actually hinted, laughing, that such was the case.
'Don't you talk with Mr Kurtz?' I said. 'You don't talk with that
man—you listen to him,' he exclaimed with severe exaltation.
'But now—' He waved his arm, and in the twinkling of an eye
was in the uttermost depths of despondency. In a moment he
came up again with a jump, possessed himself of both my hands,
shook them continuously, while he gabbled: 'Brother sailor . . .
honour . . . pleasure . . . delight . . . introduce myself . . . Russian
. . . son of an archpriest . . . Government of Tambov . . . What?
Tobacco! English tobacco; the excellent English tobacco! Now,
that's brotherly. Smoke? Where's a sailor that does not smoke?'

"The pipe soothed him, and gradually I made out he had run
away from school, had gone to sea in a Russian ship; ran away
again; served some time in English ships; was now reconciled with
the arch-priest. He made a point of that. 'But when one is young
one must see things, gather experience, ideas; enlarge the mind.'
'Here!' I interrupted. 'You can never tell! Here I have met Mr
Kurtz,' he said, youthfully solemn and reproachful. I held my
tongue after that. It appears he had persuaded a Dutch trading-
house on the coast to fit him out with stores and goods, and had
started for the interior with a light heart, and no more idea of
what would happen to him than a baby. He had been wandering
about that river for nearly two years alone, cut off from everybody and everything. 'I am not so young as I look. I am twenty-
five,' he said. 'At first old Van Shuyten would tell me to go to the
devil,' he narrated with keen enjoyment; 'but I stuck to him, and
talked and talked, till at last he got afraid I would talk the hind-
leg off his favourite dog, so he gave me some cheap things and a
few guns, and told me he hoped he would never see my face again.
Good old Dutchman, Van Shuyten. I've sent him one small lot of
ivory a year ago, so that he can't call me a little thief when I get
back. I hope he got it. And for the rest I don't care. I had some
wood stacked for you. That was my old house. Did you see?'

"I gave him Towson's book. He made as though he would kiss
me, but restrained himself. 'The only book I had left, and I
thought I had lost it,' he said, looking at it ecstatically. 'So many
accidents happen to a man going about alone, you know. Canoes
get upset sometimes—and sometimes you've got to clear out so

quick when the people get angry.' He thumbed the pages. 'You made notes in Russian?' I asked. He nodded. 'I thought they were written in cipher,' I said. He laughed, then became serious. 'I had lots of trouble to keep these people off,' he said. 'Did they want to kill you?' I asked. 'Oh no!' he cried, and checked himself. 'Why did they attack us?' I pursued. He hesitated, then said shame-facedly, 'They don't want him to go.' 'Don't they?' I said, curi-ously. He nodded a nod full of mystery and wisdom. 'I tell you,' he cried, 'this man has enlarged my mind.' He opened his arms wide, staring at me with his little blue eyes that were perfectly round."

# III

"I looked at him, lost in astonishment. There he was before me, in motley, as though he had absconded from a troupe of mimes, enthusiastic, fabulous. His very existence was improbable, inexplicable, and altogether bewildering. He was an insoluble problem. It was inconceivable how he had existed, how he had succeeded in getting so far, how he had managed to remain—why he did not instantly disappear. 'I went a little further,' he said, 'then still a little further—till I had gone so far that I don't know how I'll ever get back. Never mind. Plenty time. I can manage. You take Kurtz away quick—quick—I tell you.' The glamour of youth enveloped his particoloured rags, his destitution, his loneliness, the essential desolation of his futile wanderings. For months—for years—his life hadn't been worth a day's purchase; and there he was gallantly, thoughtlessly alive, to all appearance indestructible solely by the virtue of his few years and of his unreflecting audacity. I was seduced into something like admiration—like envy. Glamour urged him on, glamour kept him unscathed. He surely wanted nothing from the wilderness but space to breathe in and to push on through. His need was to exist, and to move onwards at the greatest possible risk, and with a maximum of privation. If the absolutely pure, uncalculating, impractical spirit of adventure had ever ruled a human being, it ruled this be-patched youth. I almost envied him the possession of this modest and clear flame. It seemed to have consumed all thought of self so completely, that, even while he was talking to you, you forgot that it was he—the man before your eyes—who had gone through these things. I did not envy him his devotion to Kurtz, though. He had not meditated over it. It came to him, and he accepted it with a sort of eager fatalism. I must say that to me it appeared about the most dangerous thing in every way he had come upon so far.

"They had come together unavoidably, like two ships becalmed near each other, and lay rubbing sides at last. I suppose Kurtz wanted an audience, because on a certain occasion, when encamped in the forest, they had talked all night, or more probably Kurtz had talked. 'We talked of everything,' he said, quite transported at the recollection. 'I forgot there was such a thing as sleep. The night did not seem to last an hour. Everything! Everything! . . . Of love too.' 'Ah, he talked to you of love!' I said, much amused. 'It isn't what you think,' he cried, almost passionately. 'It was in general. He made me see things—things.'

"He threw his arms up. We were on deck at the time, and the headman of my wood-cutters, lounging near by, turned upon him his heavy and glittering eyes. I looked around, and I don't know why, but I assure you that never, never before, did this land, this river, this jungle, the very arch of this blazing sky, appear to me so hopeless and so dark, so impenetrable to human thought, so pitiless to human weakness. 'And, ever since, you have been with him, of course?' I said.

"On the contrary. It appears their intercourse had been very much broken by various causes. He had, as he informed me proudly, managed to nurse Kurtz through two illnesses (he alluded to it as you would to some risky feat), but as a rule Kurtz wandered alone, far in the depths of the forest. 'Very often coming to this station, I had to wait days and days before he would turn up,' he said. 'Ah, it was worth waiting for!—sometimes.' 'What was he doing? exploring or what?' I asked. 'Oh yes, of course'; he had discovered lots of villages, a lake too—he did not know exactly in what direction; it was dangerous to inquire too much—but mostly his expeditions had been for ivory. 'But he had no goods to trade with by that time,' I objected. 'There's a good lot of cartridges left even yet,' he answered, looking away. 'To speak plainly, he raided the country,' I said. He nodded. 'Not alone, surely!' He muttered something about the villages round that lake. 'Kurtz got the tribe to follow him, did he?' I suggested. He fidgeted a little. 'They adored him,' he said. The tone of these words was so extraordinary that I looked at him searchingly. It was curious to see his mingled eagerness and reluctance to speak of Kurtz. The man filled his life, occupied his thoughts, swayed his emotions. 'What can you expect?' he burst out; 'he came to them with thunder and lightning, you know—and they had never seen anything like it—and very terrible. He could be very terrible.[1] You can't judge Mr Kurtz as you would an ordinary man. No, no, no! Now—just to give you an idea—I don't mind telling you, he wanted to shoot me too one day—but I don't judge him.' 'Shoot you!' I cried. 'What for?' 'Well, I had a small lot of ivory the chief of that village near my house gave me. You see I used to shoot game for them. Well, he wanted it, and wouldn't hear reason. He declared he would shoot me unless I gave him the ivory and then cleared out of the country, because he could do so, and had a fancy for it, and there was nothing on earth to prevent him killing whom he jolly well pleased. And it was true too. I gave him the ivory. What did I care! But I didn't clear out. No, no. I couldn't leave him. I had to be careful, of course, till we got friendly again for a time. He had his second illness then. Afterwards I had to keep out of the way; but I didn't mind. He was living for the most part in those villages on the lake. When he came down to the river, sometimes he would talk to me, and sometimes it was better for me to be careful. This man suffered too much. He hated all this, and somehow he couldn't get away. When I had a chance I begged him to try and leave while there was time; I offered to go back with him. And he would say yes, and then he would remain; go off on another ivory hunt; disappear for weeks; forget himself amongst these people—forget himself—you know.' 'Why! he's mad,' I said. He protested indignantly. Mr Kurtz couldn't be mad. If I had heard him talk, only two days ago, I wouldn't dare hint at such a thing. . . . I had taken up my binoculars while we talked, and was looking at the shore, sweeping the limit of the forest at each side and at the back of the house. The consciousness of there being people in that bush, so silent, so quiet—as silent and quiet as the ruined house on the hill—made me uneasy. There was no sign on the face of nature of this amazing tale that was not so much told as suggested to me in desolate exclamations, completed by shrugs, in interrupted phrases, in hints ending in deep sighs. The woods were unmoved, like a mask—heavy, like the closed door of a prison—they looked with their air of hidden knowledge, of patient expectation, of unapproachable silence. The Russian was explaining to me that it was only lately that Mr Kurtz had come down to the river, bringing along with him all the fighting men of that lake tribe. He had been absent for several months—getting himself adored, I suppose—and had come down unexpectedly, with the intention to all appearance of making a raid either across the river or down stream. Evidently the appetite for more ivory had got the better of the—what shall I say?—less material aspirations. However he had got much worse suddenly. 'I heard he was lying here helpless, and so I came up—took my chance,' said the Russian. 'Oh, he is bad, very bad.' I directed my glass to the house. There were no signs of life, but there was the ruined roof, the long mud wall peeping above the grass, with three little square window-holes, no two of the same size; all this brought within reach of my hand, as it were. And then I made a brusque movement, and one of the remaining posts of that vanished fence leaped up in the field of my glass. You remember I told you I had been struck at the distance by certain attempts at ornamentation, rather remarkable in the ruinous aspect of the place. Now I had suddenly a nearer view, and its first result was to make me throw my head back as if before a blow. Then I went carefully from post to post with my glass, and I saw my mistake. These round knobs were not ornamental but symbolic; they were expressive and puzzling, striking and disturbing—food for thought and also for the vultures if there had been any looking down from the sky; but at all events for such ants as were industrious enough to ascend the pole. They would have been even more impressive, those heads on the stakes, if their faces had not been turned to the house. Only one, the first I had made out, was facing my way. I was not so shocked as you may think. The start back I had given was really nothing but a movement of surprise. I had expected to see a knob of wood there, you know. I returned deliberately to the first I had seen—and there it was, black, dried, sunken, with closed eyelids—a head that seemed to sleep at the top of that pole, and, with the shrunken dry lips showing a narrow white line of the teeth, was smiling too, smiling continuously at some endless and jocose dream of that eternal slumber.

"I am not disclosing any trade secrets. In fact the manager said afterwards that Mr Kurtz's methods had ruined the district. I have no opinion on that point, but I want you clearly to understand that there was nothing exactly profitable in these heads being there. They only showed that Mr Kurtz lacked restraint in the

gratification of his various lusts, that there was something want-
ing in him—some small matter which, when the pressing need
arose, could not be found under his magnificent eloquence.
Whether he knew of this deficiency himself I can't say. I think the
knowledge came to him at last—only at the very last. But the
wilderness had found him out early, and had taken on him a terrible vengeance for the fantastic invasion. I think it had whispered
to him things about himself which he did not know, things of
which he had no conception till he took counsel with this great
solitude—and the whisper had proved irresistibly fascinating. It
echoed loudly within him because he was hollow at the core. . . .
I put down the glass, and the head that had appeared near enough
to be spoken to seemed at once to have leaped away from me into
inaccessible distance.

"The admirer of Mr Kurtz was a bit crestfallen. In a hurried,
indistinct voice he began to assure me he had not dared to take
these—say, symbols—down. He was not afraid of the natives;
they would not stir till Mr Kurtz gave the word. His ascendancy
was extraordinary. The camps of these people surrounded the
place, and the chiefs came every day to see him. They would
crawl. . . . 'I don't want to know anything of the ceremonies used
when approaching Mr Kurtz,' I shouted. Curious, this feeling that
came over me that such details would be more intolerable than
those heads drying on the stakes under Mr Kurtz's windows.
After all, that was only a savage sight, while I seemed at one
bound to have been transported into some lightless region of subtle horrors, where pure, uncomplicated savagery was a positive
relief, being something that had a right to exist—obviously—in
the sunshine. The young man looked at me with surprise. I suppose it did not occur to him Mr Kurtz was no idol of mine. He
forgot I hadn't heard any of these splendid monologues on, what
was it? on love, justice, conduct of life—or what not. If it had
come to crawling before Mr Kurtz, he crawled as much as the
veriest savage of them all. I had no idea of the conditions, he said:
these heads were the heads of rebels. I shocked him excessively by
laughing. Rebels! What would be the next definition I was to
hear? There had been enemies, criminals, workers—and these
were rebels. Those rebellious heads looked very subdued to me on
their sticks. 'You don't know how such a life tries a man like

Kurtz,' cried Kurtz's last disciple. 'Well, and you?' I said. 'I! I! I am a simple man. I have no great thoughts. I want nothing from anybody. How can you compare me to . . . ?' His feelings were too much for speech, and suddenly he broke down. 'I don't understand,' he groaned. 'I've been doing my best to keep him alive, and that's enough. I had no hand in all this. I have no abilities. There hasn't been a drop of medicine or a mouthful of invalid food for months here. He was shamefully abandoned. A man like this, with such ideas. Shamefully! Shamefully! I—I—haven't slept for the last ten nights. . . .'

"His voice lost itself in the calm of the evening. The long shadows of the forest had slipped down hill while we talked, had gone far beyond the ruined hovel, beyond the symbolic row of stakes. All this was in the gloom, while we down there were yet in the sunshine, and the stretch of the river abreast of the clearing glittered in a still and dazzling splendour, with a murky and overshadowed bend above and below. Not a living soul was seen on the shore. The bushes did not rustle.

"Suddenly round the corner of the house a group of men appeared, as though they had come up from the ground. They waded waist-deep in the grass, in a compact body, bearing an improvised stretcher in their midst. Instantly, in the emptiness of the landscape, a cry arose whose shrillness pierced the still air like a sharp arrow flying straight to the very heart of the land; and, as if by enchantment, streams of human beings—of naked human beings—with spears in their hands, with bows, with shields, with wild glances and savage movements, were poured into the clearing by the dark-faced and pensive forest. The bushes shook, the grass swayed for a time, and then everything stood still in attentive immobility.

"'Now, if he does not say the right thing to them we are all done for,' said the Russian at my elbow. The knot of men with the stretcher had stopped too, half-way to the steamer, as if petrified. I saw the man on the stretcher sit up, lank and with an uplifted arm, above the shoulders of the bearers. 'Let us hope that the man who can talk so well of love in general will find some particular reason to spare us this time,' I said. I resented bitterly the absurd danger of our situation, as if to be at the mercy of that atrocious phantom had been a dishonouring necessity. I could not hear a sound, but through my glasses I saw the thin arm extended commandingly, the lower jaw moving, the eyes of that apparition shining darkly far in its bony head that nodded with grotesque jerks.[2] Kurtz—Kurtz—that means 'short' in German—don't it? Well, the name was as true as everything else in his life—and death. He looked at least seven feet long. His covering had fallen off, and his body emerged from it pitiful and appalling as from a winding-sheet. I could see the cage of his ribs all astir, the bones of his arm waving. It was as though an animated image of death carved out of old ivory had been shaking its hand with menaces at a motionless crowd of men made of dark and glittering bronze. I saw him open his mouth wide—it gave him a weirdly voracious aspect, as though he had wanted to swallow all the air, all the earth, all the men before him. A deep voice reached me faintly. He must have been shouting. He fell back suddenly. The stretcher shook as the bearers staggered forward again, and almost at the same time I noticed that the crowd of savages was vanishing without any perceptible movement of retreat, as if the forest that had ejected these beings so suddenly had drawn them in again as the breath is drawn in a long aspiration.

"Some of the pilgrims behind the stretcher carried his arms—two shot-guns, a heavy rifle, and a light revolver-carbine—the thunderbolts of that pitiful Jupiter. The manager bent over him murmuring as he walked beside his head. They laid him down in one of the little cabins—just a room for a bed-place and a camp-stool or two, you know. We had brought his belated correspondence, and a lot of torn envelopes and open letters littered his bed. His hand roamed feebly amongst these papers. I was struck by the fire of his eyes and the composed languor of his expression. It was not so much the exhaustion of disease. He did not seem in pain. This Shadow looked satiated and calm, as though for the moment it had had its fill of all the emotions.

"He rustled one of the letters, and looking straight in my face said, 'I am glad.' Somebody had been writing to him about me. These special recommendations were turning up again. The volume of tone he emitted without effort, almost without the trouble of moving his lips, amazed me. A voice! a voice! It was grave, profound, vibrating, while the man did not seem capable of a whisper. However, he had enough strength in him—factitious no doubt—to very nearly make an end of us, as you shall hear directly.

"The manager appeared silently in the doorway; I stepped out at once and he drew the curtain after me. The Russian, eyed curiously by the pilgrims, was staring at the shore. I followed the direction of his glance.

"Dark human shapes could be made out in the distance, flitting indistinctly against the gloomy border of the forest, and near the river two bronze figures, leaning on tall spears, stood in the sunlight, under fantastic head-dresses of spotted skins, warlike and still in statuesque repose. And from right to left along the lighted shore moved a wild and gorgeous apparition of a woman.

"She walked with measured steps, draped in striped and fringed cloths, treading the earth proudly, with a slight jingle and flash of barbarous ornaments. She carried her head high; her hair was done in the shape of a helmet; she had brass leggins to the knee, brass wire gauntlets to the elbow, a crimson spot on her tawny cheek, innumerable necklaces of glass beads on her neck; bizarre things, charms, gifts of witch-men, that hung about her, glittered and trembled at every step. She must have had the value of several elephant tusks upon her. She was savage and superb, wild-eyed and magnificent; there was something ominous and stately in her deliberate progress. And in the hush that had fallen suddenly upon the whole sorrowful land, the immense wilderness, the colossal body of the fecund and mysterious life seemed to look at her, pensive, as though it had been looking at the image of its own tenebrous and passionate soul.

"She came abreast of the steamer, stood still, and faced us. Her long shadow fell to the water's edge. Her face had a tragic and fierce aspect of wild sorrow and of dumb pain mingled with the fear of some struggling, half-shaped resolve. She stood looking at us without a stir, and like the wilderness itself, with an air of brooding over an inscrutable purpose. A whole minute passed, and then she made a step forward. There was a low jingle, a glint of yellow metal, a sway of fringed draperies, and she stopped as if her heart had failed her. The young fellow by my side growled. The pilgrims murmured at my back. She looked at us all as if her life had depended upon the unswerving steadiness of her glance. Suddenly she opened her bared arms and threw them up rigid above her head, as though in an uncontrollable desire to touch the sky, and at the same time the swift shadows darted out on the earth, swept around on the river, gathering the steamer into a shadowy embrace. A formidable silence hung over the scene.

"She turned away slowly, walked on, following the bank, and passed into the bushes to the left. Once only her eyes gleamed back at us in the dusk of the thickets before she disappeared.

"'If she had offered to come aboard I really think I would have tried to shoot her,' said the man of patches, nervously. 'I had been risking my life every day for the last fortnight to keep her out of the house. She got in though one day and kicked up a row about those miserable rags I picked up in the storeroom to mend my clothes with. I wasn't decent. At least it must have been that, for she talked like a fury to Kurtz for an hour, pointing at me now and then. I don't understand the dialect of this tribe. Luckily for me, I fancy Kurtz felt too ill that day to care, or there would have been mischief. I don't understand. . . . No—it's too much for me. Ah, well, it's all over now.'

"At this moment I heard Kurtz's deep voice behind the curtain, 'Save me!—save the ivory, you mean. Don't tell me. Save *me*! Why, I've had to save you. You are interrupting my plans now. Sick! Sick! Not so sick as you would like to believe. Never mind. I'll carry my ideas out yet—I will return. I'll show you what can be done. You with your little peddling notions—you are interfering with me. I will return. I . . .'

"The manager came out. He did me the honour to take me under the arm and lead me aside. 'He is very low, very low,' he said. He considered it necessary to sigh, but neglected to be consistently sorrowful. 'We have done all we could for him—haven't we? But there is no disguising the fact, Mr Kurtz has done more harm than good to the Company. He did not see the time was not ripe for vigorous action. Cautiously, cautiously—that's my principle. We must be cautious yet. The district is closed to us for a time. Deplorable! Upon the whole, the trade will suffer. I don't deny there is a remarkable quantity of ivory—mostly fossil. We must save it, at all events—but look how precarious the position is—and why? Because the method is unsound.' 'Do you,' said I, looking at the shore, 'call it "unsound method"?' 'Without doubt,' he exclaimed, hotly. 'Don't you?' . . . 'No method at all,' I mur-

mured after a while. 'Exactly,' he exulted. 'I anticipated this.
Shows a complete want of judgment. It is my duty to point it out
in the proper quarters.'³ 'Oh,' said I, 'that fellow—what's his
name?—the brickmaker, will make a readable report for you.' He
appeared confounded for a moment. It seemed to me I had never
breathed an atmosphere so vile, and I turned mentally to Kurtz
for relief—positively for relief. 'Nevertheless I think Mr Kurtz *is*
a remarkable man,' I said with emphasis. He started, dropped on
me a cold heavy glance, said very quietly, 'He *was*,' and turned his
back on me. My hour of favour was over. I found myself lumped
along with Kurtz as a partisan of methods for which the time was
not ripe. I was unsound! Ah! but it was something to have at least
a choice of nightmares.⁴

"I had turned to the wilderness really, not to Mr Kurtz, who, I
was ready to admit, was as good as buried. And for a moment it
seemed to me as if I also were buried in a vast grave full of unspeakable secrets. I felt an intolerable weight oppressing my
breast, the smell of the damp earth, the unseen presence of vic-
torious corruption, the darkness of an impenetrable night. . . .
The Russian tapped me on the shoulder. I heard him mumbling
and stammering something about 'brother seaman—couldn't
conceal—knowledge of matters that would affect Mr Kurtz's
reputation.' I waited. For him evidently Mr Kurtz was not in his
grave. I suspect that for him Mr Kurtz was one of the immortals.
'Well!' said I at last, 'speak out. As it happens, I am Mr Kurtz's
friend—in a way.'

"He stated with a good deal of formality that had we not been
'of the same profession,' he would have kept the matter to himself
without regard to consequences. 'He suspected there was an ac-
tive ill-will towards him on the part of these white men that—'
'You are right,' I said, remembering a certain conversation I had
overheard. 'The manager thinks you ought to be hanged.' He
showed a concern at this intelligence which amused me at first. 'I
had better get out of the way quietly,' he said, earnestly. 'I can do
no more for Kurtz now, and they would soon find some excuse.
What's to stop them? There's a military post three hundred miles
from here.' 'Well, upon my word,' said I, 'perhaps you had better
go if you have any friends amongst the savages near by.' 'Plenty,'
he said. 'They are simple people—and I want nothing, you know.'

He stood biting his lip, then: 'I don't want any harm to happen to these whites here, but of course I was thinking of Mr Kurtz's reputation—but you are a brother seaman and—' 'All right,' said I, after a time. 'Mr Kurtz's reputation is safe with me.' I did not know how truly I spoke.

"He informed me, lowering his voice, that it was Kurtz who had ordered the attack to be made on the steamer. 'He hated sometimes the idea of being taken away—and then again . . . But I don't understand these matters. I am a simple man. He thought it would scare you away—that you would give it up, thinking him dead. I could not stop him. Oh, I had an awful time of it this last month.' 'Very well,' I said. 'He is all right now.' 'Ye-e-es,' he muttered, not very convinced apparently. 'Thanks,' said I; 'I shall keep my eyes open.' 'But quiet—eh?' he urged, anxiously. 'It would be awful for his reputation if anybody here—' I promised a complete discretion with great gravity. 'I have a canoe and three black fellows waiting not very far. I am off. Could you give me a few Martini-Henry cartridges?' I could, and did, with proper secrecy. He helped himself, with a wink at me, to a handful of my tobacco. 'Between sailors—you know—good English tobacco.' At the door of the pilot-house he turned round—'I say, haven't you a pair of shoes you could spare?' He raised one leg. 'Look.' The soles were tied with knotted strings sandal-wise under his bare feet. I rooted out an old pair, at which he looked with admiration before tucking it under his left arm. One of his pockets (bright red) was bulging with cartridges, from the other (dark blue) peeped 'Towson's Inquiry,' etc., etc. He seemed to think himself excellently well equipped for a renewed encounter with the wilderness. 'Ah! I'll never, never meet such a man again. You ought to have heard him recite poetry—his own too it was, he told me. Poetry!' He rolled his eyes at the recollection of these delights. 'Oh, he enlarged my mind!' 'Goodbye,' said I. He shook hands and vanished in the night. Sometimes I ask myself whether I had ever really seen him—whether it was possible to meet such a phenomenon! . . .

"When I woke up shortly after midnight his warning came to my mind with its hint of danger that seemed, in the starred darkness, real enough to make me get up for the purpose of having a look round. On the hill a big fire burned, illuminating fitfully a crooked corner of the station-house. One of the agents with a picket of a few of our blacks, armed for the purpose, was keeping guard over the ivory; but deep within the forest, red gleams that wavered, that seemed to sink and rise from the ground amongst confused columnar shapes of intense blackness, showed the exact position of the camp where Mr Kurtz's adorers were keeping their uneasy vigil. The monotonous beating of a big drum filled the air with muffled shocks and a lingering vibration. A steady droning sound of many men chanting each to himself some weird incantation came out from the black, flat wall of the woods as the humming of bees comes out of a hive, and had a strange narcotic effect upon my half-awake senses. I believe I dozed off leaning over the rail, till an abrupt burst of yells, an overwhelming outbreak of a pent-up and mysterious frenzy, woke me up in a bewildered wonder. It was cut short all at once, and the low droning went on with an effect of audible and soothing silence. I glanced casually into the little cabin. A light was burning within, but Mr Kurtz was not there.

"I think I would have raised an outcry if I had believed my eyes. But I didn't believe them at first—the thing seemed so impossible. The fact is I was completely unnerved by a sheer blank fright, pure abstract terror, unconnected with any distinct shape of physical danger. What made this emotion so overpowering was—how shall I define it?—the moral shock I received, as if something altogether monstrous, intolerable to thought and odious to the soul, had been thrust upon me unexpectedly. This lasted of course the merest fraction of a second, and then the usual sense of commonplace, deadly danger, the possibility of a sudden onslaught and massacre, or something of the kind, which I saw impending, was positively welcome and composing. It pacified me, in fact, so much that I did not raise an alarm.

"There was an agent buttoned up inside an ulster and sleeping on a chair on deck within three feet of me. The yells had not awakened him; he snored very slightly; I left him to his slumbers and leaped ashore. I did not betray Mr Kurtz—it was ordered I should never betray him—it was written I should be loyal to the nightmare of my choice. I was anxious to deal with this Shadow by myself alone—and to this day I don't know why I was so jealous of sharing with any one the peculiar blackness of that experience.

"As soon as I got on the bank I saw a trail—a broad trail through the grass. I remember the exultation with which I said to myself, 'He can't walk—he is crawling on all-fours—I've got him.' The grass was wet with dew. I strode rapidly with clenched fists. I fancy I had some vague notion of falling upon him and giving him a drubbing. I don't know. I had some imbecile thoughts. The knitting old woman with the cat obtruded herself upon my memory as a most improper person to be sitting at the other end of such an affair. I saw a row of pilgrims squirting lead in the air out of Winchesters held to the hip. I thought I would never get back to the steamer, and imagined myself living alone and unarmed in the woods to an advanced age.⁵ Such silly things—you know. And I remember I confounded the beat of the drum with the beating of my heart, and was pleased at its calm regularity.

"I kept to the track though—then stopped to listen. The night was very clear: a dark blue space, sparkling with dew and starlight, in which black things stood very still. I thought I could see a kind of motion ahead of me. I was strangely cocksure of everything that night. I actually left the track and ran in a wide semicircle (I verily believe chuckling to myself) so as to get in front of that stir, of that motion I had seen—if indeed I had seen anything. I was circumventing Kurtz as though it had been a boyish game.

"I came upon him, and, if he had not heard me coming, I would have fallen over him too; but he got up in time. He rose, unsteady, long, pale, indistinct, like a vapour exhaled by the earth, and swayed slightly, misty and silent before me; while at my back the fires loomed between the trees, and the murmur of many voices issued from the forest. I had cut him off cleverly; but when actually confronting him I seemed to come to my senses, I saw the danger in its right proportion. It was by no means over yet. Suppose he began to shout? Though he could hardly stand, there was still plenty of vigour in his voice. 'Go away—hide yourself,' he said, in that profound tone. It was very awful. I glanced back. We were within thirty yards from the nearest fire. A black figure stood up, strode on long black legs, waving long black arms, across the glow. It had horns—antelope horns, I think—on its head. Some sorcerer, some witch-man, no doubt: it looked fiend-like enough. 'Do you know what you are doing?' I whispered. 'Perfectly,' he answered, raising his voice for that single word: it sounded to me far off and yet loud, like a hail through a speaking-trumpet. If he makes a row we are lost, I thought to myself. This clearly was not a case for fisticuffs, even apart from the very natural aversion I had to beat that Shadow—this wandering and tormented thing. 'You will be lost,' I said—'utterly lost.' One gets sometimes such a flash of inspiration, you know. I did say the right thing, though indeed he could not have been more irretrievably lost than he was at this very moment, when the foundations of our intimacy were being laid—to endure—to endure—even to the end—even beyond.

"'I had immense plans,' he muttered irresolutely. 'Yes,' said I; 'but if you try to shout I'll smash your head with—' There was not a stick or a stone near. 'I will throttle you for good,' I corrected myself. 'I was on the threshold of great things,' he pleaded, in a voice of longing, with a wistfulness of tone that made my blood run cold. 'And now for this stupid scoundrel—' 'Your success in Europe is assured in any case,' I affirmed, steadily. I did not want to have the throttling of him, you understand—and indeed it would have been very little use for any practical purpose. I tried to break the spell—the heavy, mute spell of the wilderness—that seemed to draw him to its pitiless breast by the awakening of forgotten and brutal instincts, by the memory of gratified and monstrous passions. This alone, I was convinced, had driven him out to the edge of the forest, to the bush, towards the gleam of fires, the throb of drums, the drone of weird incantations; this alone had beguiled his unlawful soul beyond the bounds of permitted aspirations. And, don't you see, the terror of the position was not in being knocked on the head—though I had a very lively sense of that danger too—but in this, that I had to deal with a being to whom I could not appeal in the name of anything high or low. I had, even like the niggers, to invoke him—himself—his own exalted and incredible degradation. There was nothing either above or below him, and I knew it. He had kicked himself loose of the earth. Confound the man! he had kicked the very earth to pieces. He was alone, and I before him did not know whether I stood on the ground or floated in the air. I've been telling you what we said—repeating the phrases we pronounced—but what's the good? They were common everyday words—the familiar, vague sounds exchanged on every waking day of life. But what of that? They had behind them, to my mind, the terrific suggestiveness of words heard in dreams, of phrases spoken in nightmares. Soul! If anybody had ever struggled with a soul, I am the man. And I wasn't arguing with a lunatic either. Believe me or not, his intelligence was perfectly clear—concentrated, it is true, upon himself with horrible intensity, yet clear; and therein was my only chance—barring, of course, the killing him there and then, which wasn't so good, on account of unavoidable noise. But his soul was mad. Being alone in the wilderness, it had looked within itself, and, by heavens! I tell you, it had gone mad. I had—for my sins, I suppose—to go through the ordeal of looking into it myself. No eloquence could have been so withering to one's belief in mankind as his final burst of sincerity. He struggled with himself, too. I saw it—I heard it. I saw the inconceivable mystery of a soul that knew no restraint, no faith, and no fear, yet struggling blindly with itself. I kept my head pretty well; but when I had him at last stretched on the couch, I wiped my forehead, while my legs shook under me as though I had carried half a ton on my back down that hill. And yet I had only supported him, his bony arm clasped round my neck—and he was not much heavier than a child.

"When next day we left at noon, the crowd, of whose presence behind the curtain of trees I had been acutely conscious all the time, flowed out of the woods again, filled the clearing, covered the slope with a mass of naked, breathing, quivering bronze bodies. I steamed up a bit, then swung down-stream, and two thousand eyes followed the evolutions of the splashing, thumping, fiery river-demon beating the water with its terrible tail and breathing black smoke into the air.⁶ In front of the first rank, along the river, three men, plastered with bright red earth from head to foot, strutted to and fro restlessly. When we came abreast again, they faced the river, stamped their feet, nodded their horned heads, swayed their scarlet bodies; they shook towards the fierce river-demon a bunch of black feathers, a mangy skin with a pendant tail—something that looked like a dried gourd; they shouted periodically together strings of amazing words that resembled no sounds of human language; and the deep murmurs of the crowd, interrupted suddenly, were like the responses of some satanic litany.

"We had carried Kurtz into the pilot-house: there was more air there. Lying on the couch, he stared through the open shutter. There was an eddy in the mass of human bodies, and the woman with helmeted head and tawny cheeks rushed out to the very brink of the stream. She put out her hands, shouted something, and all that wild mob took up the shout in a roaring chorus of articulated, rapid, breathless utterance.

"'Do you understand this?' I asked.

"He kept on looking out past me with fiery, longing eyes, with a mingled expression of wistfulness and hate. He made no answer, but I saw a smile, a smile of indefinable meaning, appear on his colourless lips that a moment after twitched convulsively. "Do I not?" he said slowly, gasping, as if the words had been torn out of him by a supernatural power.

"I pulled the string of the whistle, and I did this because I saw the pilgrims on deck getting out their rifles with an air of anticipating a jolly lark. At the sudden screech there was a movement of abject terror through that wedged mass of bodies. "Don't! don't you frighten them away," cried someone on deck disconsolately. I pulled the string time after time. They broke and ran, they leaped, they crouched, they swerved, they dodged the flying terror of the sound. The three red chaps had fallen flat, face down on the shore, as though they had been shot dead. Only the barbarous and superb woman did not so much as flinch, and stretched tragically her bare arms after us over the sombre and glittering river.

"And then that imbecile crowd down on the deck started their little fun, and I could see nothing more for smoke.

"The brown current ran swiftly out of the heart of darkness, bearing us down towards the sea with twice the speed of our upward progress; and Kurtz's life was running swiftly too, ebbing, ebbing out of his heart into the sea of inexorable time. The manager was very placid, he had no vital anxieties now, he took us both in with a comprehensive and satisfied glance: the 'affair' had come off as well as could be wished. I saw the time approaching when I would be left alone of the party of 'unsound method.' The pilgrims looked upon me with disfavour. I was, so to speak, numbered with the dead. It is strange how I accepted this unforeseen partnership, this choice of nightmares forced upon me in the tenebrous land invaded by these mean and greedy phantoms.

"Kurtz discoursed. A voice! a voice! It rang deep to the very last. It survived his strength to hide in the magnificent folds of eloquence the barren darkness of his heart. Oh, he struggled! he struggled! The wastes of his weary brain were haunted by shadowy images now—images of wealth and fame revolving obsequiously round his unextinguishable gift of noble and lofty expression. My Intended, my ivory, my station, my career, my ideas—these were the subjects for the occasional utterances of elevated sentiments. The shade of the original Kurtz frequented the bedside of the hollow sham, whose fate it was to be buried presently in the mould of primeval earth. But both the diabolic love and the unearthly hate of the mysteries it had penetrated fought for the possession of that soul satiated with primitive emotions, avid of lying fame, of sham distinction, of all the appearances of success and power.

"Sometimes he was contemptibly childish. He desired to have kings meet him at railway-stations on his return from some ghastly Nowhere, where he intended to accomplish great things. 'You show them you have in hand something that is really profitable, and then there will be no limits to the recognition of your ability,' he would say. 'Of course you must take care of the motives—right motives—always.' The long reaches that were like one and the same reach, monotonous bends that were exactly alike, slipped past the steamer with their multitude of secular trees looking patiently after this grimy fragment of another world, the forerunner of change, of conquest, of trade, of massacres, of blessings. I looked ahead—piloting. 'Close the shutter,' said Kurtz suddenly one day; 'I can't bear to look at this.' I did so. There was a silence. 'Oh, but I will wring your heart yet!' he cried at the invisible wilderness.

"We broke down—as I had expected—and had to lie up for repairs at the head of an island. This delay was the first thing that shook Kurtz's confidence. One morning he gave me a packet of papers and a photograph—the lot tied together with a shoe-string. 'Keep this for me,' he said. 'This noxious fool' (meaning the manager) 'is capable of prying into my boxes when I am not looking.' In the afternoon I saw him. He was lying on his back with closed eyes, and I withdrew quietly, but I heard him mutter, 'Live rightly, die, die . . .' I listened. There was nothing more. Was he rehearsing some speech in his sleep, or was it a fragment of a phrase from some newspaper article? He had been writing for the papers and meant to do so again, 'for the furthering of my ideas. It's a duty.'

"His was an impenetrable darkness. I looked at him as you peer down at a man who is lying at the bottom of a precipice where the sun never shines. But I had not much time to give him, because I was helping the engine-driver to take to pieces the leaky cylinders, to straighten a bent connecting-rod, and in other such matters. I lived in an infernal mess of rust, filings, nuts, bolts, spanners, hammers, ratchet-drills—things I abominate, because I don't get on with them. I tended the little forge we fortunately had aboard; I toiled wearily in a wretched scrap-heap—unless I had the shakes too bad to stand.

"One evening coming in with a candle I was startled to hear him say a little tremulously, 'I am lying here in the dark waiting for death.' The light was within a foot of his eyes. I forced myself to murmur, 'Oh, nonsense!' and stood over him as if transfixed.

"Anything approaching the change that came over his features I have never seen before, and hope never to see again. Oh, I wasn't touched. I was fascinated. It was as though a veil had been rent. I saw on that ivory face the expression of sombre pride, of ruthless power, of craven terror—of an intense and hopeless despair.[7] Did he live his life again in every detail of desire, temptation, and surrender during that supreme moment of complete knowledge? He cried in a whisper at some image, at some vision—he cried out twice, a cry that was no more than a breath—

"'The horror! The horror!'

"I blew the candle out and left the cabin. The pilgrims were dining in the mess-room, and I took my place opposite the manager, who lifted his eyes to give me a questioning glance, which I successfully ignored. He leaned back, serene, with that peculiar smile of his sealing the unexpressed depths of his meanness. A continuous shower of small flies streamed upon the lamp, upon the cloth, upon our hands and faces. Suddenly the manager's boy put his insolent black head in the doorway, and said in a tone of scathing contempt—

"'Mistah Kurtz—he dead.'[8]

"All the pilgrims rushed out to see. I remained, and went on with my dinner. I believe I was considered brutally callous. However, I did not eat much. There was a lamp in there—light, don't you know—and outside it was so beastly, beastly dark. I went no more near the remarkable man who had pronounced a judgment upon the adventures of his soul on this earth. The voice was gone. What else had been there? But I am of course aware that next day the pilgrims buried something in a muddy hole.

"And then they very nearly buried me.

"However, as you see, I did not go to join Kurtz there and then. I did not. I remained to dream the nightmare out to the end, and to show my loyalty to Kurtz once more. Destiny. My destiny! Droll thing life is—that mysterious arrangement of merciless logic for a futile purpose. The most you can hope from it is some knowledge of yourself—that comes too late—a crop of unextinguishable regrets. I have wrestled with death. It is the most unexciting contest you can imagine. It takes place in an impalpable greyness, with nothing underfoot, with nothing around, without spectators, without clamour, without glory, without the great desire of victory, without the great fear of defeat, in a sickly atmosphere of tepid scepticism, without much belief in your own right, and still less in that of your adversary. If such is the form of ultimate wisdom, then life is a greater riddle than some of us think it to be. I was within a hair's-breadth of the last opportunity for pronouncement, and I found with humiliation that probably I would have nothing to say. This is the reason why I affirm that Kurtz was a remarkable man. He had something to say. He said it. Since I had peeped over the edge myself, I understand better the meaning of his stare, that could not see the flame of the candle, but was wide enough to embrace the whole universe, piercing enough to penetrate all the hearts that beat in the darkness. He had summed up—he had judged. 'The horror!' He was a remarkable man. After all, this was the expression of some sort of belief; it had candour, it had conviction, it had a vibrating note of revolt in its whisper, it had the appalling face of a glimpsed truth—the strange commingling of desire and hate. And it is not my own extremity I remember best—a vision of greyness without form filled with physical pain, and a careless contempt for the evanescence of all things—even of this pain itself. No! It is his extremity that I seem to have lived through. True, he had made that last stride, he had stepped over the edge, while I had been permitted to draw back my hesitating foot. And perhaps in this is the whole difference; perhaps all wisdom, and all truth, and all sincerity, are just compressed into that inappreciable moment of time in which we step over the threshold of the Invisible. Perhaps! I like to think that my summing-up would not have been a word of careless contempt. Better his cry—much better. It was an affirmation, a moral victory paid for by innumerable defeats, by abominable terrors, by abominable satisfactions. But it was a victory! That is why I have remained loyal to Kurtz to the last, and even beyond, when a long time after I heard once more, not his own voice, but the echo of his magnificent eloquence thrown to me from a soul as translucently pure as a cliff of crystal.

"No, they did not bury me, though there is a period of time which I remember mistily, with a shuddering wonder, like a passage through some inconceivable world that had no hope in it and no desire. I found myself back in the sepulchral city resenting the sight of people hurrying through the streets to filch a little money from each other, to devour their infamous cookery, to gulp their unwholesome beer, to dream their insignificant and silly dreams. They trespassed upon my thoughts. They were intruders whose knowledge of life was to me an irritating pretence, because I felt so sure they could not possibly know the things I knew. Their bearing, which was simply the bearing of commonplace individuals going about their business in the assurance of perfect safety,[9] was offensive to me like the outrageous flauntings of folly in the face of a danger it is unable to comprehend. I had no particular desire to enlighten them, but I had some difficulty in restraining myself from laughing in their faces, so full of stupid importance. I daresay I was not very well at that time. I tottered about the streets—there were various affairs to settle—grinning bitterly at perfectly respectable persons.[10] I admit my behaviour was inexcusable, but then my temperature was seldom normal in these days. My dear aunt's endeavours to 'nurse up my strength' seemed altogether beside the mark. It was not my strength that wanted nursing, it was my imagination that wanted soothing. I kept the bundle of papers given me by Kurtz, not knowing exactly what to do with it. His mother had died lately, watched over, as I was told, by his Intended. A clean-shaved man, with an official manner and wearing gold-rimmed spectacles, called on me one day and made inquiries, at first circuitous, afterwards suavely pressing, about what he was pleased to denominate certain 'documents.' I was not surprised, because I had had two rows with the manager on the subject out there. I had refused to give up the smallest scrap out of that package, and I took the same attitude with the spectacled man. He became darkly menacing at last, and with much heat argued that the Company had the right to every bit of information about its 'territories.' And, said he, 'Mr Kurtz's knowledge of unexplored regions must have been necessarily extensive and peculiar—owing to his great abilities and to the deplorable circumstances in which he had been placed: therefore—' I assured him Mr Kurtz's knowledge, however extensive, did not bear upon the problems of commerce or administration. He invoked then the name of science. 'It would be an incalculable loss if,' etc., etc. I offered him the report on the 'Suppression of Savage Customs,' with the postscriptum torn off. He took it up eagerly, but ended by sniffing at it with an air of contempt. 'This is not what we had a right to expect,' he remarked. 'Expect nothing else,' I said. 'There are only private letters.' He withdrew upon some threat of legal proceedings, and I saw him no more; but another fellow, calling himself Kurtz's cousin, appeared two days later, and was anxious to hear all the details about his dear relative's last moments. Incidentally he gave me to understand that Kurtz had been essentially a great musician. 'There was the making of an immense success,' said the man, who was an organist, I believe, with lank grey hair flowing over a greasy coat-collar. I had no reason to doubt his statement; and to this day I am unable to say what was Kurtz's profession, whether he ever had any—which was the greatest of his talents. I had taken him for a painter who wrote for the papers, or else for a journalist who could paint—but even the cousin (who took snuff during the interview) could not tell me what he had been—exactly. He was a universal genius—on that point I agreed with the old chap, who thereupon blew his nose noisily into a large cotton handkerchief and withdrew in senile agitation, bearing off some family letters and memoranda without importance. Ultimately a journalist anxious to know something of the fate of his 'dear colleague' turned up. This visitor informed me Kurtz's proper sphere ought to have been politics 'on the popular side.' He had furry straight eyebrows, bristly hair cropped

short, an eye-glass on a broad black ribbon, and, becoming ex-
pansive, confessed his opinion that Kurtz really couldn't write a
bit—'but heavens! how that man could talk! He electrified large
meetings. He had the faith—don't you see?—he had the faith. He
could get himself to believe anything—anything.[11] He would have
been a splendid leader of an extreme party.' 'What party?' I asked.
'Any party,' answered the other. 'He was an—an—extremist.' Did
I not think so? I assented. Did I know, he asked, with a sudden
flash of curiosity, 'what it was that had induced him to go out
there?' 'Yes,' said I, and forthwith handed him the famous Report
for publication, if he thought fit. He glanced through it hurriedly,
mumbling all the time, judged 'it would do,' and took himself off
with this plunder.

"Thus I was left at last with a slim packet of letters and the
girl's portrait. She struck me as beautiful—I mean she had a beautiful expression. I know that the sunlight can be made to lie too,
yet one felt that no manipulation of light and pose could have
conveyed the delicate shade of truthfulness upon those features.
She seemed ready to listen without mental reservation, without
suspicion, without a thought for herself. I concluded I would go
and give her back her portrait and those letters myself. Curiosity?
Yes; and also some other feeling perhaps. All that had been
Kurtz's had passed out of my hands: his soul, his body, his station,
his plans, his ivory, his career. There remained only his memory
and his Intended—and I wanted to give that up too to the past, in
a way—to surrender personally all that remained of him with me
to that oblivion which is the last word of our common fate. I don't
defend myself. I had no clear perception of what it was I really
wanted. Perhaps it was an impulse of unconscious loyalty, or the
fulfilment of one of these ironic necessities that lurk in the facts
of human existence. I don't know. I can't tell. But I went.

"I thought his memory was like the other memories of the dead
that accumulate in every man's life—a vague impress on the brain
of shadows that had fallen on it in their swift and final passage;
but before the high and ponderous door, between the tall houses
of a street as still and decorous as a well-kept alley in a cemetery,
I had a vision of him on the stretcher, opening his mouth vora-
ciously, as if to devour all the earth with all its mankind. He lived
then before me; he lived as much as he had ever lived—a shadow

insatiable of splendid appearances, of frightful realities; a shadow
darker than the shadow of the night, and draped nobly in the folds
of a gorgeous eloquence. The vision seemed to enter the house
with me—the stretcher, the phantom-bearers, the wild crowd of
obedient worshippers, the gloom of the forests, the glitter of the
reach between the murky bends, the beat of the drum, regular
and muffled like the beating of a heart—the heart of a conquering
darkness. It was a moment of triumph for the wilderness, an invading and vengeful rush which, it seemed to me, I would have to
keep back alone for the salvation of another soul. And the memory of what I had heard him say afar there, with the horned shapes
stirring at my back, in the glow of fires, within the patient woods,
those broken phrases came back to me, were heard again in their
ominous and terrifying simplicity. I remembered his abject plead-
ing, his abject threats, the colossal scale of his vile desires, the
meanness, the torment, the tempestuous anguish of his soul. And
later on I seemed to see his collected languid manner, when he
said one day, 'This lot of ivory now is really mine. The Company
did not pay for it. I collected it myself at a very great personal risk.
I am afraid they will try to claim it as theirs though. H'm. It is a
difficult case. What do you think I ought to do—resist? Eh? I
want no more than justice.' . . . He wanted no more than justice—
no more than justice. I rang the bell before a mahogany door on
the first floor, and while I waited he seemed to stare at me out of
the glassy panel—stare with that wide and immense stare embrac-
ing, condemning, loathing all the universe. I seemed to hear the
whispered cry, 'The horror! The horror!'

"The dusk was falling. I had to wait in a lofty drawing-room
with three long windows from floor to ceiling that were like three
luminous and bedraped columns. The bent gilt legs and backs of
the furniture shone in indistinct curves. The tall marble fireplace
had a cold and monumental whiteness. A grand piano stood mas-
sively in a corner, with dark gleams on the flat surfaces like a
sombre and polished sarcophagus. A high door opened—closed.
I rose.

"She came forward, all in black, with a pale head, floating towards me in the dusk. She was in mourning. It was more than a
year since his death, more than a year since the news came; she
seemed as though she would remember and mourn for ever. She

took both my hands in hers and murmured, 'I had heard you were coming.' I noticed she was not very young—I mean not girlish. She had a mature capacity for fidelity, for belief, for suffering.[12] The room seemed to have grown darker, as if all the sad light of the cloudy evening had taken refuge on her forehead. This fair hair, this pale visage, this pure brow, seemed surrounded by an ashy halo from which the dark eyes looked out at me. Their glance was guileless, profound, confident, and trustful. She carried her sorrowful head as though she were proud of that sorrow, as though she would say, I—I alone know how to mourn for him as he deserves. But while we were still shaking hands, such a look of awful desolation came upon her face that I perceived she was one of those creatures that are not the playthings of Time. For her he had died only yesterday. And, by Jove! the impression was so powerful that for me too he seemed to have died only yesterday— nay, this very minute. I saw her and him in the same instant of time—his death and her sorrow—I saw her sorrow in the very moment of his death. Do you understand? I saw them together— I heard them together. She had said, with a deep catch of the breath, 'I have survived'; while my strained ears seemed to hear distinctly, mingled with her tone of despairing regret, the sum- ming-up whisper of his eternal condemnation. I asked myself what I was doing there, with a sensation of panic in my heart as though I had blundered into a place of cruel and absurd mysteries not fit for a human being to behold. She motioned me to a chair. We sat down. I laid the packet gently on the little table, and she put her hand over it. . . . 'You knew him well,' she murmured, after a moment of mourning silence.

"'Intimacy grows quick out there,' I said. 'I knew him as well as it is possible for one man to know another.'

"'And you admired him,' she said. 'It was impossible to know him and not to admire him. Was it?'

"'He was a remarkable man,' I said, unsteadily. Then before the appealing fixity of her gaze, that seemed to watch for more words on my lips, I went on, 'It was impossible not to—'

"'Love him,' she finished eagerly, silencing me into an appalled dumbness. 'How true! how true! But when you think that no one knew him so well as I! I had all his noble confidence. I knew him best.'

"'You knew him best,' I repeated. And perhaps she did. But with every word spoken the room was growing darker, and only her forehead, smooth and white, remained illumined by the unextinguishable light of belief and love.

"'You were his friend,' she went on. 'His friend,' she repeated, a little louder. 'You must have been, if he had given you this, and sent you to me. I feel I can speak to you—and oh! I must speak. I want you—you who have heard his last words—to know I have been worthy of him. . . . It is not pride. . . . Yes! I am proud to know I understood him better than any one on earth—he told me so himself. And since his mother died I have had no one—no one—to—to—'

"I listened. The darkness deepened. I was not even sure whether he had given me the right bundle. I rather suspect he wanted me to take care of another batch of his papers which, after his death, I saw the manager examining under the lamp. And the girl talked, easing her pain in the certitude of my sympathy; she talked as thirsty men drink. I had heard that her engagement with Kurtz had been disapproved by her people. He wasn't rich enough or something. And indeed I don't know whether he had not been a pauper all his life. He had given me some reason to infer that it was his impatience of comparative poverty that drove him out there.

"'. . . Who was not his friend who had heard him speak once?' she was saying. 'He drew men towards him by what was best in them.' She looked at me with intensity. 'It is the gift of the great,' she went on, and the sound of her low voice seemed to have the accompaniment of all the other sounds, full of mystery, desolation, and sorrow, I had ever heard—the ripple of the river, the soughing of the trees swayed by the wind, the murmurs of wild crowds, the faint ring of incomprehensible words cried from afar, the whisper of a voice speaking from beyond the threshold of an eternal darkness. 'But you have heard him! You know!' she cried.

"'Yes, I know,' I said with something like despair in my heart, but bowing my head before the faith that was in her, before that great and saving illusion that shone with an unearthly glow in the darkness, in the triumphant darkness from which I could not have defended her—from which I could not even defend myself.

"'What a loss to me—to us!'—she corrected herself with beautiful generosity; then added in a murmur, 'To the world.' By the last gleams of twilight I could see the glitter of her eyes, full of tears—of tears that would not fall.

"'I have been very happy—very fortunate—very proud,' she went on. 'Too fortunate. Too happy for a little while. And now I am unhappy for—for life.'

"She stood up; her fair hair seemed to catch all the remaining light in a glimmer of gold.[13] I rose too.

"'And of all this,' she went on, mournfully, 'of all his promise, and of all his greatness, of his generous mind, of his noble heart, nothing remains—nothing but a memory. You and I—'

"'We shall always remember him,' I said, hastily.

"'No!' she cried. 'It is impossible that all this should be lost—that such a life should be sacrificed to leave nothing—but sorrow. You know what vast plans he had. I knew of them too—I could not perhaps understand—but others knew of them. Something must remain. His words, at least, have not died.'

"'His words will remain,' I said.

"'And his example,' she whispered to herself. 'Men looked up to him—his goodness shone in every act. His example—'

"'True,' I said; 'his example too. Yes, his example. I forgot that.'

"'But I do not. I cannot—I cannot believe—not yet. I cannot believe that I shall never see him again, that nobody will see him again, never, never, never!'

"She put out her arms as if after a retreating figure, stretching them black and with clasped pale hands across the fading and narrow sheen of the window. Never see him! I saw him clearly enough then. I shall see this eloquent phantom as long as I live, and I shall see her too, a tragic and familiar Shade, resembling in this gesture another one, tragic also, and bedecked with powerless charms, stretching bare brown arms over the glitter of the infernal stream, the stream of darkness. She said suddenly very low, 'He died as he lived.'

"'His end,' said I, with dull anger stirring in me, 'was in every way worthy of his life.'

"'And I was not with him,' she murmured. My anger subsided before a feeling of infinite pity.

"'Everything that could be done—' I mumbled.

"'Ah, but I believed in him more than any one on earth—more

than his own mother, more than—himself. He needed me! Me! I would have treasured every sigh, every word, every sign, every glance.'

"I felt like a chill grip on my chest. 'Don't,' I said, in a muffled voice.

"'Forgive me. I—I—have mourned so long in silence—in silence. . . . You were with him—to the last? I think of his loneliness. Nobody near to understand him as I would have understood. Perhaps no one to hear . . .'

"'To the very end,' I said, shakily. 'I heard his very last words. . . .' I stopped in a fright.

"'Repeat them,' she said in a heart-broken tone. 'I want—I want—something—something—to—to live with.'

"I was on the point of crying at her, 'Don't you hear them?' The dusk was repeating them in a persistent whisper all around us, in a whisper that seemed to swell menacingly like the first whisper of a rising wind. 'The horror! the horror!'

"'His last word—to live with,' she murmured. 'Don't you understand I loved him—I loved him—I loved him!'

"I pulled myself together and spoke slowly.

"'The last word he pronounced was—your name.'

"I heard a light sigh, and then my heart stood still, stopped dead short by an exulting and terrible cry, by the cry of inconceivable triumph and of unspeakable pain. 'I knew it—I was sure!' . . . She knew. She was sure. I heard her weeping; she had hidden her face in her hands. It seemed to me that the house would collapse before I could escape, that the heavens would fall upon my head. But nothing happened. The heavens do not fall for such a trifle. Would they have fallen, I wonder, if I had rendered Kurtz that justice which was his due? Hadn't he said he wanted only justice? But I couldn't. I could not tell her. It would have been too dark—too dark altogether. . . ."

Marlow ceased, and sat apart, indistinct and silent, in the pose of a meditating Buddha. Nobody moved for a time. "We have lost the first of the ebb," said the Director, suddenly. I raised my head. The offing was barred by a black bank of clouds, and the tranquil waterway leading to the uttermost ends of the earth flowed sombre under an overcast sky—seemed to lead into the heart of an immense darkness.

# Afterword

Not long after Chinua Achebe published his coruscating 1977 essay "An Image of Africa," assailing *Heart of Darkness* as "an offensive and totally deplorable book," an African American college student named Barack Obama was challenged by his friends to explain why he was reading "this racist tract."[1] "Because . . . ," Obama stammered, "because the book teaches me things. . . . about white people, I mean. See, the book's not really about Africa. Or black people. It's about the man who wrote it. The European. The American. A particular way of looking at the world."[2]

Discussions of *Heart of Darkness* have long circled around these two resonant interpretations of what, and where, the "heart of darkness" might be. Some readers, starting in Conrad's day with the founders of the Congo Reform Association, immediately recognized Conrad's "heart of darkness" as a representation of the "Dark Continent" of Africa. For them *Heart of Darkness* was (for good or ill) primarily a document about a specific place, the Congo Free State, and a specific historical phenomenon, colonialism. Others, however, understood *Heart of Darkness* to be a meditation on something internal to the human psyche and thus transcending specific historical conditions. Obama's comment traced a line that reached all the way back to Conrad's friend Edward Garnett, who called *Heart of Darkness* "the acutest analysis of the deterioration of the white man's *morale*, when he is let loose from European restraint."[3]

Yet between the novel's concrete observations about Congo and its evocation of a universal "horror," Conrad planted markers of other places, other histories, and other actors. It's a novel "about" Africa set in the Thames estuary; it's a novel "about" imperialism whose most explicit references to conquest are to

Roman invaders and Elizabethan freebooters. It's a novel "about" an interior psychological condition that's obsessed with the mechanics of describing it to others—Kurtz's fiancée, the men on the *Nellie*, and, of course, the reader.

These aspects of *Heart of Darkness* invite a fresh interpretation that situates the book *between* the highly specific conditions of Congo in Conrad's day and the highly abstract meanings that have been applied to it. Set in the context of Conrad's own life and world, *Heart of Darkness* stands out as a meditation on the consolidation of the global order whose lineaments we have inherited today.

How exactly a Polish sea captain named Konrad Korzeniowski ended up on a steamboat on the Congo River—let alone writing a novel about it in English—depended on a set of political, technological, and economic conditions that marked a step change in the extent of what would now be called globalization. Ocean-going steamships and transcontinental railroads carried immigrants from Europe and Asia in numbers never seen before or since. Undersea telegraph cables transmitted news, for the first time in history, faster than people. London became the center of a global financial market that was more integrated during Conrad's lifetime than it would be again till the 1980s. A handful of imperial powers planted their flags in so much of the world's territory that by 1900 the only continent left for claiming was Antarctica—while a host of international organizations harmonized time zones, longitude, and weights and measures. International laws were developed to set norms and manage conflicts—and even, in 1885, to delineate and recognize a new, putatively independent country. It was called the Congo Free State.[4]

Conrad wouldn't have known the word "globalization," but his life course embodied it. Born in Ukraine in 1857, Conrad spent his childhood in the shadow of Russian oppression when his parents, fervent Polish nationalists, were exiled for their political activism. Orphaned at eleven, when he was sixteen Conrad ran as far away from the Russian Empire as he could, by traveling to Marseille to become a sailor.

For the next twenty years, on long-haul journeys to the Caribbean, Australia, and southeast Asia, Conrad traced firsthand the networks of trade and migration that linked up the world. It was as a sailor that he first came to Britain, which had far and away the world's largest fleet; and it was on board ships that Conrad, in his twenties, started learning English—his third language, after Polish and French. Making his home in London between voyages, Conrad settled in a country that was unusually open to immigrants and free from the political persecution that had blighted his childhood. In 1886, he proudly cemented a new identity by becoming a certified master (captain) in the British merchant marines, and a naturalized British citizen.

Conrad's maritime career also carried him across a period of technological disruption. Transoceanic steamships were steadily displacing sailing ships, rendering a whole set of skills—and the people who had them—obsolete. To most of Conrad's European peers, the steamship was an engine of progress: the bringer of "civilization" into hitherto little-trafficked parts of the world. But during a formative few months in 1887 on a steamship running between Singapore and Borneo, Conrad developed a contrasting impression. The "monotonous huckster's round" took him into zones of piracy, slave-trading, and smuggling, and carried him up river estuaries peopled by "human outcasts such as one finds in the lost corners of the world."[5] Conrad came to see the difference between sail and steam as the difference between better and worse ways of life. In his fiction he idealized sail as a "craft," fostering a distinctive sense of community and ethics. The steamship, by contrast, spelled dehumanization, artlessness, isolation, and corruption. When he returned from southeast Asia, he began translating what he'd seen into his first novel, *Almayer's Folly* (1894), about a washed-up white trader on a river in Borneo.

Conrad's trip to Congo in 1890 was an aberration in a maritime career spent overwhelmingly on British sailing ships and in Australasia. Though he later claimed that traveling to Africa had been a childhood dream, in fact, Conrad took the gig on the *Roi des Belges* partly because he couldn't find anything better. He got the job thanks to serendipity: A Polish relative in Brussels gave him an entrée to the company; he interviewed for it using his fluent French; and his British master's certificate provided the all-important credentials. Every aspect of his strikingly international life prepared him for it.

---

Conrad arrived in the Congo Free State carrying impressions and attitudes he'd shaped all over the world. He saw overseas imperialism through eyes opened by the Russian Empire. He witnessed the assertion of "civilization" by steamship through eyes skeptical about its benefits. And he surveyed a tropical river through eyes imprinted by the estuaries of Borneo.

Details from Conrad's diary of his overland trek up the rapids to Stanley Pool (Kinshasa) would make their way nearly verbatim into *Heart of Darkness*—but another record of his engagement with the river may be traced in the pages of a different manuscript he carried with him, the draft of his first novel, *Almayer's Folly*. The novel's fifth chapter, composed in Africa or soon after Conrad's return, resonates with details from the "Up-River Book" in which Conrad had registered details of the river's course, current, and depth. "Steer for the big green branch," he wrote. Moor where "a great log had stranded . . . at right angles to the bank, forming a kind of jetty." Reach up to a hanging branch and push under "a low archway of thickly matted creepers giving access to a miniature bay." He noted a sunrise breaking through the "white canopy of mist . . . disclosing the wrinkled surface of the river sparkling," and observed "black clouds and heavy showers" rolling in from a distance, "the angry river under the lash of the thunderstorm, sweeping onward towards the sea."[6]

Conrad's fictional revisiting of Congo in *Heart of Darkness* also came as a brief interruption within years spent engaging with the sea and with southeast Asia. His first two novels and a projected third were all set in the Malay Archipelago, as was a short story he wrote in the summer of 1898, "Youth," narrated by an old salt named Charles Marlow. "You see how Malays cling to me!" Conrad told a confidante. "I am devoted to Borneo."[7] At the end of 1898, running short of money, he set aside his latest southeast Asian novel to write *Heart of Darkness*—and as soon as he finished it, he picked up yet another manuscript set on a steamship in Asia, and introduced the character of Marlow, fresh from *Heart of Darkness*, as its narrator. The result grew into his 1900 novel *Lord Jim*.

This Conradian habit of continental drift, with ideas and observations formed in one location merging into stories set in others, accounts for Conrad's narrative masterstroke in *Heart of Darkness*. As the rivers of Borneo flow into the Congo, the Congo flows into the Thames. By nesting Marlow's experience in Africa inside the telling of his tale in London, Conrad turned what happened "over there" into a statement about what was going on right *here*. It located the "heart of darkness" no less in Africa than in London, the hub of global trade and finance, driven by the very sorts of men who listen to Marlow on the *Nellie*: a company director, a lawyer, and an accountant.

When the Thames reminds Marlow of the Congo, he isn't simply saying, look, Africa is more primitive than England. He's saying that history is like a river. You can go up or you can go down. You can ride the current to get ahead, but the same force can push you back, the way the same river that carried the conquistadors out had led the Roman invaders in. What happened "over there" has already happened here, Marlow warns, and maybe it can happen again. Anyone can be savage. Everywhere can go dark.

A perceptive contemporary reviewer noted how "the 'going Fantee' of civilised man, has been treated often enough in fiction, but never has the 'why of it' been appreciated by any author as Mr. Conrad here appreciates it, and never . . . has any writer till now succeeded in bringing . . . it all home to sheltered folk."[8] Conrad's meditations on progress and civilization resonate afresh in the early twenty-first century, as readers ponder anew the consequences of globalization. For all that *Heart of Darkness* shows Conrad to have been in some stereotypical respects a man of his times, in its engagement with the blowback of empire and globalization, it also reveals him to be an uncanny prophet of our own.

MAYA JASANOFF

# Notes to the Afterword

1. Chinua Achebe, "An Image of Africa," *The Massachusetts Review* 18, no. 4 (December 1, 1977), pp. 788, 790.
2. Barack Obama, *Dreams from My Father*, rev. ed. (New York: Three Rivers Press, 2004), pp. 102–3.
3. Unsigned review by Edward Garnett from "Mr. Conrad's New Book," *Academy and Literature* (December 6, 1902), pp. 606–7.
4. I base this paragraph on, among others: Eric Hobsbawm, *The Age of Empire* (New York: Vintage Books, 1989); A. G. Hopkins, ed., *Globalization in World History* (New York: W. W. Norton, 2002); C. A. Bayly, *The Birth of the Modern World, 1780–1914: Global Connections and Comparisons* (Malden, MA: Blackwell Publishing, 2004); Adam McKeown, "Global Migration, 1846–1940," *Journal of World History*, vol. 15, no. 2 (June 2004): 155–89; Jürgen Osterhammel and Niels P. Petersson, *Globalization: A Short History*, trans. Dona Geyer (Princeton: Princeton University Press, 2005); John Darwin, *After Tamerlane: The Rise and Fall of Global Empires, 1400–2000* (New York: Bloomsbury, 2009); Mark Mazower, *Governing the World: The History of an Idea* (New York: The Penguin Press, 2012); Jürgen Osterhammel, *The Transformation of the World: A Global History of the Nineteenth Century*, trans. Patrick Camiller (Princeton: Princeton University Press, 2014); Vanessa Ogle, *The Global Transformation of Time, 1870–1950* (Cambridge: Harvard University Press, 2015); Charles S. Maier, *Once Within Borders: Territories of Power, Wealth, and Belonging since 1500* (Cambridge: Harvard University Press, 2016).
5. Joseph Conrad to Marguerite Poradowska, August 1894, in Frederick Karl and Laurence Davies, eds., *The Collected Letters of Joseph Conrad*, vol. 1 (Cambridge, UK: Cambridge University Press, 1983), p. 171.
6. For the composition history of the manuscript, see the Cambridge critical edition: Joseph Conrad, *Almayer's Folly*, ed. Floyd Eugene Eddleman and David Leon Higdon (Cambridge, UK:

Cambridge University Press, 1994), pp. 159–65. Quotes from chapter 5, pp. 52–57.

7. Joseph Conrad to Marguerite Poradowska, August 1894, in *Collected Letters*, p. 171.

8. Unsigned review by Hugh Clifford in *The Spectator*, in Keith Carabine, ed. *Joseph Conrad: Critical Assessments*, vol. 1 (Mountfield, near Robertsbridge, East Sussex: Helm Information, 1992), p. 295.

# Filmography

## ADAPTATIONS OF *HEART OF DARKNESS*

*Apocalypse Now Redux*. Dir. Francis Ford Coppola. Perf. Marlon Brando and Martin Sheen. 1979.

*Heart of Darkness*. Dir. Nicolas Roeg. Perf. Tim Roth and John Malkovich. 1994.

*Hearts of Darkness: A Filmmaker's Apocalypse*. Dir. Fax Bahr, George Hickenlooper, Eleanor Coppola. 1991.

## ADAPTATIONS OF OTHER CONRAD WORKS

*Lord Jim*. Dir. Richard Brooks. Perf. Peter O'Toole and James Mason. 1965.

*Nostromo*. Dir. Alastair Reid. Perf. Colin Firth and Albert Finney. 1997.

*The Secret Agent*. Dir. Christopher Hampton. Perf. Bob Hoskins and Robin Williams. 1996.

*Swept from the Sea*. Dir. Beeban Kidron. Perf. Ian McKellen and Rachel Weisz. 1997.

*Victory*. Dir. Mark Peploe. Perf. Willem Dafoe and Sam Neill. 1996.

## FILMS ABOUT AFRICA

*The African Queen*. Dir. John Huston. Perf. Humphrey Bogart and Katharine Hepburn. 1951.

*Amistad*. Dir. Steven Spielberg. Perf. Morgan Freeman, Anthony Hopkins, and Djimon Hounsou. 1997.

*Babel*. Dir. Alejandro González Iñárritu. Perf. Brad Pitt and Cate Blanchett. 2006.

*La Battaglia di Algeri (The Battle of Algiers)*. Dir. Gillo Pontecorvo. Perf. Jean Martin. 1966.

*Black Hawk Down*. Dir. Ridley Scott. Perf. Josh Hartnett and Ewan McGregor. 2001.

*Blood Diamond*. Dir. Edward Zwick. Perf. Leonardo DiCaprio, Djimon Hounsou, and Jennifer Connelly. 2006.

*Congo*. Dir. Frank Marshall. Perf. Laura Linney and Dylan Walsh. 1995.

*The Constant Gardener*. Dir. Fernando Meirelles. Perf. Ralph Fiennes and Rachel Weisz. 2005.

*Cry Freedom*. Dir. Richard Attenborough. Perf. Kevin Kline and Denzel Washington. 1987.

*Darfur Now* (documentary). Dir. Ted Braun. Perf. Don Cheadle. 2007.

*The Ghost and the Darkness*. Dir. Stephen Hopkins. Perf. Michael Douglas and Val Kilmer. 1996.

*Hotel Rwanda*. Dir. Terry George. Perf. Don Cheadle. 2004.

*King Leopold's Ghost* (documentary). Dir. Pippa Scott and Oreet Rees. 2006.

*King Solomon's Mines*. Dir. Andrew Marton and Compton Bennett. Perf. Deborah Kerr. 1950.

*King Solomon's Mines*. Dir. Robert Stevenson. Perf. Paul Robeson. 1937.

*King Solomon's Mines*. Dir. J. Lee Thompson. Perf. Richard Chamberlain. 1985.

*The Last King of Scotland*. Dir. Kevin Macdonald. Perf. Forest Whitaker and James McAvoy. 2006.

*Lumumba*. Dir. Raoul Peck. Perf. Eriq Ebouaney. 2000.

*Mogambo*. Dir. John Ford. Perf. Clark Gable, Ava Gardner, and Grace Kelly. 1953.

*Out of Africa*. Dir. Sydney Pollack. Perf. Meryl Streep and Robert Redford. 1985.

*The Snows of Kilimanjaro*. Dir. Henry King. Perf. Gregory Peck, Susan Hayward, and Ava Gardner. 1952.

*Tears of the Sun*. Dir. Antoine Fuqua. Perf. Bruce Willis and Monica Bellucci. Sony Pictures, 2003.

*Tsotsi*. Dir. Gavin Hood. Perf. Presley Chweneyagae. 2005.

# FILMS ABOUT IMPERIALISM

*Burn!* Dir. Gillo Pontecorvo. Perf. Marlon Brando. 1969.

*Gandhi.* Dir. Richard Attenborough. Perf. Ben Kingsley. 1982.

*Lawrence of Arabia.* Dir. David Lean. Perf. Peter O'Toole. 1962.

*The Man Who Would Be King.* Dir. John Huston. Perf. Sean Connery and Michael Caine. 1975.

*A Passage to India.* Dir. David Lean. Perf. Judy Davis and Alec Guinness. 1984.

# Telling Africa's Story Today: Recent Films About Africa

While opinions differ about just how forward-looking the publication of *Heart of Darkness* was in its time—some critics and readers appreciate the work as a bold statement against imperialism, while others think Conrad did not go far enough—the work has had a significant impact on portrayals of Africa in fiction and nonfiction alike for more than a century. In this brief essay, I will explore the connections between Conrad's portrayal of Africa in *Heart of Darkness* and a number of films released in recent years: *Hotel Rwanda* (2004), *The Constant Gardener* (2005), *Tsotsi* (2005), *The Last King of Scotland* (2006), and *Blood Diamond* (2006).

In three films featuring major Hollywood stars released within the last decade, the story of Africa has continued to be told through the viewpoint primarily of white characters from the West. Each offers a skeptical look at whether change can really occur, often exploring the possibility through distinct portrayals of gender. In *The Constant Gardener*, a tale primarily of corporate greed in Africa, Ralph Fiennes's diplomat Justin Quayle at first rejects and then ultimately embraces the forceful efforts of his activist wife, Tessa (Rachel Weisz), to uncover the exploitation of Africans by a fictional European pharmaceutical company. In *The Last King of Scotland*, James McAvoy's Scottish doctor Nicholas Garrigan is starstruck and largely oblivious to the violent tactics of his employer Idi Amin while his friend Sarah Merrit, a doctor's wife herself, works diligently and quietly to provide proper care to a small village. And in *Blood Diamond*, Leonardo DiCaprio's soldier-turned-diamond-smuggler Danny Archer struggles to overcome his self-interest, urged to more noble aspirations by the Western journalist Maddy Bowen (Jennifer Connelly) and Mende fisherman Solomon Vandy (Djimon Hounsou). These are also each partially fictionalized accounts of Africa, much like *Heart of Darkness*, that explore and offer similarly ambiguous lessons about whether intervention in Africa—be it to exploit or to save— is a positive thing.

In contrast, two other films tell stories that are more about Africa than about the West. *Hotel Rwanda* (2004) recounts the tale of Paul Rusesabagina, a hotel owner who successfully managed to protect more than a thousand Rwandans from the genocide of 1994. It exposes as absurd the minute differences upon which this genocide was based, pondering the ironies of Africa, but it certainly also aims to expose a Western audience to the fact that the West could have but did not intervene (the question of United Nations intervention in particular is a central feature of the story). But a film released only a year later, *Tsotsi*, based on a South African novel about an orphan-turned-thug who accidentally kidnaps a baby, offers a tale that could be told in virtually any language or country where classes are divided by wealth and opportunity.

More than a century after Conrad introduced a deeply troubled Africa to the Western world, modern films continue to explore similar questions in often complex ways. But unlike *Heart of Darkness*, women are now featured prominently and Africans speak for themselves. The answers may still be beyond us, but the countless voices of Africans and those who seek to help Africans can now be heard.

# Contemporary Reviews of
## *Heart of Darkness*

### EDWARD GARNETT

Unsigned review from "Mr. Conrad's New Book,"
*Academy and Literature* (6 December 1902): 606–07.

The publication in volume form of Mr. Conrad's three stories, "Youth," "Heart of Darkness," "The End of the Tether," is one of the events of the literary year. These stories are an achievement in art which will materially advance his growing reputation. Of the stories, "Youth" may be styled a modern English epic of the Sea; "The End of the Tether" is a study of an old sea captain who, at the end of forty years' trade exploration of the Southern seas, finding himself dispossessed by the perfected routine of the British empire overseas he has helped to build, falls on evil times, and faces ruin calmly, fighting to the last. These two will be more popular than the third, "Heart of Darkness," a study of "the white man in Africa" which is most amazing, a consummate piece of artistic *diablerie*. On reading "Heart of Darkness" on its appearance in *Blackwood's Magazine* our first impression was that Mr. Conrad had, here and there, lost his way. Now that the story can be read, not in parts, but from the first page to the last at a sitting, we retract this opinion and hold "Heart of Darkness" to be the high-water mark of the author's talent. It may be well to analyse this story a little so that the intelligent reader, reading it very deliberately, may see better for himself why Mr. Conrad's book enriches English literature.

"Heart of Darkness," to present its theme bluntly, is an impression, taken from life, of the conquest by the European whites of a certain portion of Africa, an impression in particular of the civilising methods of a certain great European Trading Company

face to face with the "nigger." We say this much because the English reader likes to know where he is going before he takes art
seriously, and we add that he will find the human life, black and
white, in "Heart of Darkness" an uncommonly and uncannily
serious affair. If the ordinary reader, however, insists on taking
the subject of a tale very seriously, the artist takes his method of
presentation more seriously still, and rightly so. For the art of
"Heart of Darkness"—as in every psychological masterpiece—
lies in the relation of the things of the spirit to the things of the
flesh, of the invisible life to the visible, of the sub-conscious life
within us, our obscure motives and instincts, to our conscious
actions, feelings and outlook. Just as landscape art implies the
artist catching the exact relation of a tree to the earth from which
it springs, and of the earth to the sky, so the art of "Heart of
Darkness" implies the catching of infinite shades of the white
man's uneasy, disconcerted, and fantastic relations with the ex-
ploited barbarism of Africa; it implies the acutest analysis of the
deterioration of the white man's *morale*, when he is let loose from
European restraint, and planted down in the tropics as an "emissary of light" armed to the teeth, to make trade profits out of the
"subject races." The weirdness, the brilliance, the psychological
truth of this masterly analysis of two Continents in conflict, of the
abysmal gulf between the white man's system and the black man's
comprehension of its results, is conveyed in a rapidly rushing narrative which calls for close attention on the reader's part. But the
attention once surrendered, the pages of the narrative are as enthralling as the pages of Dostoevsky's *Crime and Punishment*.
The stillness of the sombre African forests, the glare of sunshine,
the feeling of dawn, of noon, of night on the tropical rivers, the
isolation of the unnerved, degenerating whites staring all day and
every day at the Heart of Darkness which is alike meaningless and
threatening to their own creed and conceptions of life, the helpless
bewilderment of the unhappy savages in the grasp of their flabby
and rapacious conquerors—all this is a page torn from the life of
the Dark Continent—a page which has been hitherto carefully
blurred and kept away from European eyes. There is no "intention" in the story, no *parti pris*, no prejudice one way or the other;
it is simply a piece of art, fascinating and remorseless, and the
artist is but intent on presenting his sensations in that sequence
and arrangement whereby the meaning or the meaninglessness of

the white man in uncivilised Africa can be felt in its really significant aspects. If the story is too strong meat for the ordinary reader, let him turn to "Youth," wherein the song of every man's youth is indeed sung. [. . .] Mr. Conrad is easily among the first writers of to-day. His special individual gift, as an artist, is of so placing a whole scene before the reader that the air, the landscape, the moving people, the houses on the quays, the ships in the harbour, the sounds, the scents, the voices in the air, all fuse in the perfect and dream-like illusion of an unforgettable reality.

Unsigned review from the *Manchester Guardian*
(10 December 1902): 3.

Mr. Joseph Conrad's latest volume, *Youth*, contains three stories, of which the one that gives the title is the shortest. This and the second one may be regarded as a kind of sequence. The third and longest, "The End of the Tether," is admirable, but in comparison with the others the tension is relaxed. It is in a manner more deliberate, less closely packed; this is Conrad, but not Conrad in his fine frenzy; it gives an engaging picture of a noble old man, pathetic, imaginative, deserving a whole array of eulogistic adjectives, but it is not of the amazing quality of Mr. Conrad at his best. The other two, though not of such scope and design, are of the quality of *Lord Jim*—that is to say, they touch the high-water mark of English fiction and continue a great expression of adventure and romance. Both stories follow Mr. Conrad's particular convention; they are the outpourings of Marlow's experiences. It would be useless to pretend that they can be very widely read. Even to those who are most impressed an excitement so sustained and prolonged, in which we are braced to encounter so much that menaces and appals, must be something of a strain. "Youth," in this conception of Mr. Conrad's, is not the time of freedom and delight, but "the test, the trial of life." No labour is too great, no danger is too close for this great adventure of the spirit.

"Heart of Darkness" is, again, the adventure of youth, an adventure more significant than the mere knockabout of the world. It is youth in the toils, a struggle with phantoms worse than the elements, "a weary pilgrimage amongst hints for nightmares," a destructive experience.

It must not be supposed that Mr. Conrad makes attack upon col-
onisation, expansion, even upon Imperialism. In no one is the
essence of the adventurous spirit more instinctive. But cheap ide-
als, platitudes of civilisation are shrivelled up in the heat of such
experiences. The end of this story brings us back to the familiar,
reassuring region of common emotions, to the grief and constancy
of the woman who had loved Kurtz and idealises his memory. It
shows us how far we have travelled.

Those who can read these two stories in sympathy with Mr.
Conrad's temperament will find in them a great expression of the
world's mystery and romance. They show the impact upon an
undaunted spirit of what is terrible and obscure; they are adventure in terms of experience; they represent the sapping of life that
cannot be lived on easy terms. Mr. Conrad's style is his own—
concentrated, tenacious, thoughtful, crammed with imaginative
detail, breathless, yet missing nothing. Its grim earnestness bends
to excursions of irony, to a casual humour, dry, subdued to its
surroundings. Phrases strike the mind like lines of verse; we weary
under a tension that is never slackened. He is one of the greatest
of sea-writers and the most subjective of them. His storms are not
the picturesque descriptions of the great phenomena, we see them
in the "weary, serious faces," in the dreadful concentration of the
actors. Mr. Conrad is intensely human and, we may add with
some pride of fellowship, intensely modern. By those who seek for
the finest expositions of the modern spirit "Youth" and "Heart of
Darkness" cannot be neglected.

Unsigned review from the *Times Literary Supplement* 48
(12 December 1902): 372.

Telling tales, just spinning yarns, has gone out of fashion since the
novel has become an epitome of everything a man has to say about
anything. The three stories in *Youth* by Joseph Conrad are in this
reference a return to an earlier taste. The yarns are of the sea, told
with an astonishing zest; and given with vivid accumulation of
detail and iterative persistency of emphasis of the quality of character and scenery. The method is exactly the opposite of Mr.
Kipling's. It is a little precious; one notes a tasting of the quality
of phrases and an occasional indulgence in poetic rhetoric. But the

effect is not unlike Mr. Kipling's. In the first story, "Youth," the colour, the atmosphere of the East is brought out as in a picture. The concluding scene of the "Heart of Darkness" is crisp and brief enough for Flaubert, but the effect—a woman's ecstatic belief in a villain's heroism—is reached by an indulgence in the picturesque horror of the villain, his work and his surroundings, which is pitiless in its insistence, and quite extravagant according to the canons of art. But the power, the success in conveying the impression vividly, without loss of energy is undoubted and is refreshing. "The End of the Tether," the last of the three, is the longest and best. Captain Whalley is racy of the sea, and an embodiment of its finest traditions; and the pathos of his long-drawn wrestle with the anger of circumstance is poignant to the end. Mr. Conrad should have put him in the forefront of the book. There are many readers who would not get beyond the barren and not very pretty philosophy of "Youth"; more who might feel they had had enough horror at the end of "The Heart of Darkness." But they would miss a great deal if they did not reach "The End of the Tether." It has this further advantage over the other two tales, that it is much less clever, much less precious.

Unsigned review from *Athenaeum* (20 December 1902): 824.

The art of Mr. Conrad is exquisite and very subtle. He uses the tools of his craft with the fine, thoughtful delicacy of a mediaeval clockmaker. [. . .] Putting aside all considerations of mere taste, one may say at once that Mr. Conrad's methods command and deserve the highest respect, if only by reason of their scholarly thoroughness. One feels that nothing is too minute, no process too laborious for this author. He considers not material rewards, but the dignity of his work, of all work. [. . .]

A critical writer has said that all fiction may roughly be divided into two classes: that dealing with movement and adventure, and the other dealing with characterization, the analysis of the human mind. In the present, as in every one of his previous books, Mr. Conrad has stepped outside these boundaries, and made his own class of work as he has made his own methods. All his stories have movement and incident, most of them have adventure, and the motive in all has apparently been the careful analysis, the philosophic presentation, of phases of human character. His studious and minute drawing of the action of men's minds, passions, and principles forms fascinating reading. But he has another gift of which he himself may be less conscious, by means of which his other more incisive and purely intellectual message is translated for the proper understanding of simpler minds and plainer men. That gift is the power of conveying atmosphere, and in the exercise of this talent Mr. Conrad has few equals among our living writers of fiction. He presents the atmosphere in which his characters move and act with singular fidelity, by means of watchful and careful building in which the craftsman's methods are never obtrusive, and after turning the last page of one of his books we rise saturated by the very air they breathed. This is a great power, but, more or less, it is possessed by other talented writers of fiction. The rarity of it in Mr. Conrad lies in this, that he can surround both his characters and his readers with the distinctive atmosphere of a particular story within the limits of a few pages. This is an exceptional gift, and the more to be prized in Mr. Conrad for the reason that he shows some signs of growing oversubtle in his analysis of moods, temperaments, and mental idiosyncrasies. It is an extreme into which all artists whose methods are delicate, minute and searching are apt to be led. We have at least one other analyst of temperament and mood in fiction whose minute subtlety, scrupulous restraint, and allusive economy of words resemble Mr. Conrad's. And, becoming an obsession, these characteristics tend to weary the most appreciative reader. With Mr. Conrad, however, these rather dangerous intellectual refinements are illumined always by a vivid wealth of atmosphere, and translated simply by action, incident, strong light and shade, and distinctive colouring. [. . .]

The reviewer deliberately abstains both from quotation and from any attempt at analysis of a story like "The Heart of Darkness." Any such attempt in a limited space would be a painful injustice where work of this character is concerned. Further, the reader is warned that this book cannot be read understandingly— as evening newspapers and railway novels are perused—with one mental eye closed and the other roving. Mr. Conrad himself spares no pains, and from his readers he demands thoughtful attention. He demands so much, and, where the intelligent are concerned, we think he will command it.

# Further Reading

## CRITICAL STUDIES

Adams, David. *Colonial Odysseys: Empire and Epic in the Modernist Novel.* Ithaca: Cornell University Press, 2003.

Caminero-Santangelo, Byron. *African Fiction and Joseph Conrad: Reading Postcolonial Intertextuality.* Albany: State University of New York Press, 2005.

Carabine, Keith, and Max Saunders, eds. *Inter-Relations: Conrad, James, Ford and Others.* Boulder: Social Science Monographs; Lublin: Maria Curie-Skłodowska University; New York: Distributed by Columbia University Press, 2003.

Cooper, Brenda. *Weary Sons of Conrad: White Fiction Against the Grain of Africa's Dark Heart.* New York: Peter Lang, 2002.

Donovan, Stephen. *Joseph Conrad and Popular Culture.* Basingstoke [England]; New York: Palgrave Macmillan, 2005.

Henricksen, Bruce. *Nomadic Voices: Conrad and the Subject of Narrative.* Urbana, Ill.: University of Illinois Press, 1992.

Kaplan, Carola M., Peter Mallios, and Andrea White, eds. *Conrad in the Twenty-First Century: Contemporary Approaches and Perspectives.* New York: Routledge, 2005.

Lange, Attie de, Gail Fincham, and Wiesław Krajka, eds. *Conrad in Africa: New Essays on "Heart of Darkness."* (New York: Columbia University Press, 2002.

Sherry, Norman. *Conrad: A Critical Heritage.* London: Routledge and Kegan Paul, 1973.

White, Andrea. *Joseph Conrad and the Adventure Tradition.* Cambridge: Cambridge University Press, 1993.

White, Harry, and Irving L. Finston. "The Two River Narratives in *Heart of Darkness*" and "Who Put Kurtz on the Congo?" *Conra-*

*diana: A Journal of Joseph Conrad Studies,* vol. 42, no. 1–2, Spring/
Summer, 2010.

## NINETEENTH-CENTURY ACCOUNTS
## OF AFRICA

Hobson, J. A. *Imperialism: A Study.* London: Unwin Hyman, 1988.
Kingsley, Mary. *Travels in West Africa.* London: The Folio Society,
1976.
Morel, E. D. *Great Britain and the Congo: The Pillage of the Congo
Basin.* New York: H. Fertig, 1969.
Park, Mungo. *Travels in the Interior Districts of Africa.* Durham, N.C.:
Duke University Press, 2000.
Stanley, Henry Morton. *How I Found Livingstone.* Vercelli: White Star,
2006.

## CONRAD'S CONTEMPORARIES

Ford, Ford Madox. *The Good Soldier: A Tale of Passion.* London; New
York: Penguin Classics, 2007.
Haggard, H. Rider. *King Solomon's Mines.* London; New York: Pen-
guin Classics, 2007.
———. *She.* London; New York: Penguin Classics, 2001.
Kipling, Rudyard. *Kim.* New York: Penguin, 1987.
Kucich, John, ed. *Fictions of Empire* (includes Kipling's "The Man Who
Would Be King" and Robert Louis Stevenson's *The Beach of
Falesá*). Boston: Houghton Mifflin, 2003.

## CONRAD'S INFLUENCE

Achebe, Chinua. *Arrow of God.* Garden City, N.Y.: Anchor Books,
1969.
———. *No Longer at Ease.* Oxford: Heinemann, 1987.
———. *Things Fall Apart.* New York: Anchor Books, 1994.
Aidoo, Ama Ata. *Our Sister Killjoy.* London: Longman, 1977.
Boyd, William. *A Good Man in Africa.* London: H. Hamilton, 1981.
———. *An Ice-Cream War.* New York: Vintage Books, 1982.

Boyle, T. C. *Water Music*. Boston: Little, Brown, 1981.

Coetzee, J. M. *Waiting for the Barbarians*. New York: Penguin, 1999.

Fitzgerald, F. Scott. *The Great Gatsby*. New York: Scribner, 2000.

Foden, Giles. *The Last King of Scotland*. New York: Vintage Books, 1999.

Forster, E. M. *A Passage to India*. New York: Penguin, 2005.

Garland, Alex. *The Beach*. New York: Riverhead Books, 1997.

Golding, William. *Lord of the Flies*. New York: Penguin, 1999.

Gordimer, Nadine. *July's People*. New York: Penguin Books, 1982.

Kerouac, Jack. *On the Road*. New York: Penguin Books, 2005.

Naipaul, V. S. *A Bend in the River*. New York: Vintage International, 1989.

Ngugi wa Thiong'o. *A Grain of Wheat*. London: Heinemann Educational, 1986.

———. *Moving the Centre: The Struggle for Cultural Freedoms*. London: J. Currey; Portsmouth, N.H.: Heinemann, 1993.

Orwell, George. *Burmese Days*. New York: Harcourt, Brace & World, 1962.

Silverberg, Robert. *Downward to the Earth*. Garden City, N.Y.: Doubleday, 1970.

Warren, Robert Penn. *All the King's Men*. New York: Harcourt, 2001.

## RELATED HISTORICAL BOOKS

Arendt, Hannah. *Eichmann in Jerusalem: A Report on the Banality of Evil*. New York: Penguin Books, 2006.

Browning, Christopher R. *Ordinary Men: Reserve Police Battalion 101 and the Final Solution in Poland*. New York: HarperPerennial, 1998.

Butcher, Tim. *Blood River: A Journey to Africa's Broken Heart*. London: Chatto & Windus, 2007. (Retraces Conrad's journey up the Congo.)

Easterly, William. *The White Man's Burden: Why the West's Efforts to Aid the Rest Have Done So Much Ill and So Little Good*. New York: Penguin Press, 2006.

Edgerton, Robert. *The Troubled Heart of Africa: A History of the Congo*. New York: St. Martin's Press, 2002.

French, Howard W. *A Continent for the Taking: The Tragedy and Hope of Africa*. New York: Knopf, 2004.

Hochschild, Adam. *King Leopold's Ghost: A Story of Greed, Terror, and Heroism in Colonial Africa.* Boston: Houghton Mifflin, 1998.

Klee, Ernst, Willi Dressen, and Volker Reiss, eds. *The Good Old Days: The Holocaust as Seen by Its Perpetrators and Bystanders.* New York: Free Press, 1991.

Mealer, Bryan. *All Things Must Fight to Live: Stories of War and Deliverance in Congo.* New York: Bloomsbury; Distributed in the trade by Macmillan, 2008.

Otis, Laura, ed. *Literature and Science in the Nineteenth Century: An Anthology.* New York: Oxford University Press, 2002.

Pakenham, Thomas. *The Scramble for Africa: White Man's Conquest of the Dark Continent from 1876–1912.* New York: Random House, 1991.

Reader, John. *Africa: A Biography of the Continent.* New York: Vintage Books, 1999.

Stearns, Jason K. *Dancing in the Glory of Monsters: The Collapse of the Congo and the Great War of Africa.* New York: Public Affairs, 2011.

Wrong, Michela. *In the Footsteps of Mr. Kurtz: Living on the Brink of Disaster in Mobutu's Congo.* New York: HarperCollins Publishers, 2001.

# Character Sketches

*Heart of Darkness* features a substantial number of unnamed characters, many of whom also share similar characteristics, adding to the potential confusion. In fact, only two characters of significance are named—the story's most important figures, Kurtz and Charlie Marlow (also named are Fresleven, the deceased captain whom Marlow replaces aboard the Congo steamer he pilots; Towson/Towser, the author of the sailor's manual that Marlow discovers shortly before arriving at the Inner Station; and Van Shuyten, a Dutch trader on the Congo coast who equips the harlequin for his journey into the Congo). What follows are primarily brief descriptions of the various unnamed individuals whom Marlow meets on his voyage up the river.

**Marlow's audience:** Marlow tells his tale to a group of his friends aboard a boat floating below London on the Thames. The group includes the unnamed first narrator, the Director of Companies, the Lawyer, and the Accountant. The latter three, in addition to being closely related to individuals whom Conrad often spent time with, were all involved daily with the British economy, including its connections with imperial activity in places like Africa and India. And, in this way, they very much reflect the people who would have been reading *Heart of Darkness* in *Blackwood's Magazine*: English businessmen of the middle and upper classes. Once Marlow begins his tale, however, they are barely referenced, aside from a few brief moments in which Marlow responds to their objections or doubts about his tale.

**The Accountant:** This is the first of a series of workers for the Company whom Marlow encounters and describes in extensive and often withering detail. The accountant works at the Outer Station (corresponding to Matadi in real life). There he maintains an astonishingly formal level of dress, with starched shirts, a jacket, and a necktie among his attire (which he owes to the "native women" whom he has taught to launder his clothes). His method of coping with the uncertainties of the Congo is to focus his attention almost solely on the proper accounting of the Company's funds, which leads to his brutal complaint about a dying man's groans interrupting his all-important calculations. Marlow is both impressed and disgusted by "this miracle," as he describes him.

**The Manager:** This is the man in charge of the Central Station (corresponding to Kinshasa). During an initial interview as well as his time at the Central Station and later during the journey up the Congo to recover Kurtz, Marlow learns a fair amount of information about the manager, little of which he likes. The manager, who is "commonplace" in virtually every respect and who does not inspire respect but instead "uneasiness," apparently blames Kurtz for taking his place in the pecking order of the Company. Immensely proud of his ability to survive while many other Europeans are killed by "various tropical diseases," he famously announces, "Men who come out here should have no entrails." Indeed, the manager and his uncle both believe that the manager can ultimately gain the promotion he wishes if he simply stays alive. But they may also be helping Kurtz to die by wrecking the steamboat that Marlow is to command (the evidence in the text is not conclusive but certainly hints at this possibility) and denying him supplies. Once Kurtz has been recovered and shortly before his death, the manager cannot resist expressing how he *knew* that Kurtz would come to this kind of end. On the whole, Marlow finds the manager's hypocritical and self-interested behavior to be nauseating and extremely troubling, yet also representative of the kinds of "workers" that the Company ultimately creates.

**The Brickmaker:** Perhaps the shrewdest of the Company employees whom Marlow meets, the brickmaker is a substantial source of information about Kurtz and the ongoing intrigues among the Company men. He doesn't actually make bricks, but he does give Marlow a more complete understanding of who Kurtz is, at least in terms of the Company. At the same time, the brickmaker also reveals a pettiness and a paranoia that certainly echo the manager's beliefs. Marlow is hardly impressed, calling him a "papier-mâché

Mephistopheles"—essentially, a troublemaker whose words are no more meaningful than any others he has heard from other imperialists. Told that he and Kurtz are members of the "new gang of virtue," Marlow decides to have a bit of fun with the brickmaker, allowing him to believe that Marlow is closely allied with Kurtz and that he will make the brickmaker's life hard should Kurtz's ascendancy through the Company continue. The brickmaker, who apparently hoped to be Assistant Manager under the General Manager of the Central Station, is perhaps the novel's best example of what T. S. Eliot would later call "the hollow men."

The Fireman: One of only two Africans aboard the steamboat whom Marlow specifically describes, the fireman maintains the boiler on the craft. Marlow's description of him is an uneven mix of appreciation and condescension, as he speaks of the fireman as "an improved specimen" who was often "hard at work, a thrall to strange witchcraft, full of improving knowledge." At the same time, though, Marlow brutally explains (perhaps trying to cater to racist views among his audience) "to look at him was as edifying as seeing a dog in a parody of breeches and a feather hat, walking on his hind-legs." Ultimately, while Marlow cannot quite move beyond the racist views of his time, he does seem to appreciate the fireman's devotion to the work that must be done aboard the steamboat.

The Helmsman: Unlike the fireman, whom Marlow only briefly describes, Marlow ultimately points to a more substantial and real bond between himself and the helmsman of the Congo steamer he captains. At first, though, Marlow paints the helmsman as an inconsistent and attention-hungry fool. Once the attack commences, the helmsman reacts by stamping his feet in an animalistic way. Frustrated by the noise and commotion that the helmsman makes, Marlow expresses a growing frustration with him. But everything changes as Marlow slowly realizes (much like his discovery of the arrows) that the helmsman has been mortally wounded by a spear (he sees the look on his face, he feels the warm liquid around his feet, and then he finally sees the fatal wound). Forced to watch this young African die and to witness the haunting look on his face, Marlow reassesses his relationship with the helmsman, ultimately telling his audience, "I am not prepared to affirm the fellow [Kurtz] was exactly worth the life we lost in getting to him." Despite his bigoted response to the helmsman's outward behavior, Marlow's posthumous appreciation of him seems more akin to a captain personally mourning the loss of one of his crew, no matter what his race.

**The Harlequin/Russian:** This man—who is called a number of things: the harlequin, the Russian, Kurtz's disciple—has been Kurtz's closest companion during his months of violent pillaging of the local villages near the station. He greets Marlow as the steamer arrives at the Inner Station (near Stanley Falls)[1] shortly after the attack. Marlow also discovers that the writing that he took to be ciphers in the seamanship manual that he found near Kurtz's station was, in fact, Russian penned by the harlequin himself. The harlequin wears a large coat that has been patched many times with different colors of cloth, thus appearing similar to the multicolored map of Africa that Marlow glimpsed much earlier in the story. Above all, the harlequin is an unrepentant and fully devoted disciple of Kurtz, ready to defend any of his actions. In this way, he deeply unnerves Marlow, who only partially realizes that, by retelling the story of Kurtz and refusing to condemn him, he may be more like the Russian than he realizes—maybe even Kurtz's last disciple himself.

---

1 For updated scholarship see Harry White and Irving L. Finston, "The Two River Narratives in 'Heart of Darkness'" and "Who Put Kurtz on the Congo?" *Conradiana: A Journal of Joseph Conrad Studies* 42:1–2, Spring/Summer, 2010.

# Notes

## PART I

1. *the biggest, and the greatest, town on earth*: In 1890, London was the largest city in the world (and would continue to be until about 1925), with approximately five million inhabitants. It was also the world's busiest port throughout the eighteenth and nineteenth centuries, with numerous docks lining the river Thames for miles.

2. *The Lawyer*: With only a few notable exceptions (particularly Marlow and Kurtz), Conrad avoids assigning proper names to his characters in *Heart of Darkness*. In the case of Marlow's immediate audience aboard the ship, this was likely to increase any identification Conrad's readers would have had with the men of business and industry aboard. For the Company men in Africa, Conrad may have wanted to avoid identifying them too closely with real individuals he encountered during his time in the Congo, or he may have simply sought to emphasize how little Marlow knows and understands of these individuals. The Nobel Prize–winning author J. M. Coetzee uses a similar approach in his novel *Waiting for the Barbarians* (1980), naming neither his protagonist nor the empire for which he works.

3. *The water shone pacifically; the sky, without a speck, was a benign immensity of unstained light; the very mist on the Essex marshes was like a gauzy and radiant fabric, hung from the wooded rises inland, and draping the low shores in diaphanous folds*: Descriptions of nature like these occur throughout many of Conrad's works and show a significant connection to impressionist works of art by famous painters, including Claude Monet. This impressionistic technique in fiction is also a hallmark of several well-known modernist writers, including Virginia Woolf.

4. *What greatness had not floated on the ebb of that river into the mystery of an unknown earth! ... The dreams of men, the seed of commonwealths, the germs of empires*: In contrast to Marlow's

skeptical approach, the first narrator displays an unchecked enthusiasm for British imperial endeavors. In this way, he reflects the attitudes of most professional Englishmen of the time, many of whom read *Blackwood's Magazine*, the journal in which *Heart of Darkness* was first published. It is also quite ironic that the first of three installments of *Heart of Darkness* was the first and most prominent piece in the magazine's special issue of its thousandth edition, which was specifically devoted to celebrating British imperialism.

5. *Marlow*: Most critics credit Conrad's invention of Charlie Marlow as a pivotal device that allowed the author finally to "find his voice." After several awkward attempts at omniscient or shifting perspectives in his first few novels, Conrad, with Marlow as his narrator, speaks with a single and clear voice. Marlow's first appearance actually occurs in *Lord Jim*, a novel that Conrad began writing before *Heart of Darkness* (though it wasn't published serially until after *Heart of Darkness*). Conrad also used Marlow as his narrator in two other works, *Youth* (1902) and *Chance* (1913).

6. *"the hate"*: In this crucial early paragraph in his narrative, Marlow offers up two "Roman" figures who point directly to two central characters of the African tale he is about to tell: The military officer who endures the harsh climate in the hopes of gaining promotion and a glorious return to Rome seems to match quite well with the manager who travels with Marlow to reclaim Kurtz. And the "decent young citizen" who has squandered his money and hopes to redeem himself suggests the man at the heart of Marlow's tale, Kurtz himself.

7. *"The conquest of the earth, which mostly means the taking it away from those who have a different complexion or slightly flatter noses than ourselves, is not a pretty thing when you look into it too much"*: This passage points directly to a term later coined by Sigmund Freud, the "narcissism of minor differences." In essence, Freud argued that humans release their greatest violence against those more similar to them than different, because that very similarity represents a greater threat to identity (see "The Taboo of Virginity" [1917] and *Civilization and Its Discontents* [1930]). Hauntingly, this notion remains all too real in Africa, as was especially apparent during the Rwandan genocide of 1994 (the minute difference between the Hutus and the Tutsis, the two warring ethnic groups, is made especially clear in a memorable scene from the 2004 film *Hotel Rwanda*).

8. *"What redeems it is the idea only. An idea at the back of it; not a*

*sentimental pretence but an idea; and an unselfish belief in the idea—something you can set up, and bow down before, and offer a sacrifice to . . .*": Though it had been engaged in imperial activity for a number of decades (particularly in India), Britain and its European rivals did not aggressively pursue expansions of their imperial claims until roughly the last fifteen years of the nineteenth century, in the wake of the famous Berlin Conference. Because of the increased competition, "imperialism" took on a more nationalistic and jingoistic importance, and often became "Imperialism" instead. Also note Marlow's ellipses here; they appear fairly frequently throughout his narrative and remind us that often what he *doesn't* say is at least as significant as what he *does*.

9. "*I have been in some of them, and . . . well, we won't talk about that*": Conrad's time as a seaman brought him a fairly substantial "dose of the East." Ships that he served aboard made regular stops in the Australian ports of Adelaide, Sydney, and Melbourne, while his travels also brought him to places such as Singapore, Bangkok, Calcutta (now Kolkata), and the comparatively small and exotic port of Berau on the east coast of Borneo. This small port is particularly important, however, because it was here that he met Charles William Olmeijer, the inspiration for his first novel, *Almayer's Folly*.

10. "*I went on along Fleet Street*": Fleet Street was long the home of Britain's most important and influential newspapers. Today the newspapers have largely moved elsewhere, and the numerous law offices along Fleet Street make it important to London's legal community.

11. "*'in the interests of science'*": Phrenology, a now disproven science that claimed to be able to predict mental characteristics based on the shape of the skull, was a popular idea that helped support a number of racist beliefs in the Victorian era (and fostered some of the thinking behind eugenics as well). Interestingly, and more positively, it also served as an early precursor of modern cognitive sciences that pursue explanations for certain behaviors by examining brain activity.

12. "*'interesting for science to watch the mental changes of individuals, on the spot'*": Though still in its relative infancy, the field of anthropology, led by the work of Franz Boas and Bronisław Malinowski around the turn of the twentieth century, increasingly came to favor the idea of extended experiences and observations in the field as the best means to understand the full context of the cultures or groups being studied.

13. "*'Are you an alienist?'*": In his popular novel *The Alienist* (1994),

Caleb Carr resurrects this nineteenth-century term and concept by telling a story that anticipates television's *CSI* series but that is set in 1896 New York City.

14. *"I felt as though, instead of going to the centre of a continent, I were about to set off for the centre of the earth"*: Conrad here makes an obvious connection to one of Jules Verne's most famous works, *Journey to the Center of the Earth*. Verne wrote about environments even more alien than the Congo of *Heart of Darkness*, but he also contributed greatly to the success of adventure fiction as a genre. The endurance of Verne's tale continues, as is made apparent by the film version of the story released in the summer of 2008 and starring Brendan Fraser.

15. *"Black rags were wound round their loins, and the short ends behind wagged to and fro like tails"*: There are a number of moments like this in *Heart of Darkness* that seem to point directly (even deliberately) to the writings of Charles Darwin, whose *On the Origin of Species* (1859) and especially *The Descent of Man* (1871) popularized ideas about evolution and the survival of the fittest that were already "in the air" during the 1840s and '50s. The "tails" that Marlow mentions here offer a brief but nonetheless racist hint that these Africans are less evolved beings.

16. *"They passed me within six inches, without a glance, with that complete, deathlike indifference of unhappy savages"*: Jean-Jacques Rousseau, one of the eighteenth century's most significant philosophers, often posited the idea that those who were most removed from "civilization" were best able to live in a purely happy state. He also believed that there was a purity to such lives and also spoke of "noble" savages that lived beyond the corrupt and ignoble "civilized" world.

17. *"'To make money, of course'"*: J. A. Hobson argued in his 1902 work *Imperialism* that Britain's imperial actions were largely driven by a relatively small group of businessmen who were also in large part the beneficiaries of the British Empire. At the same time, one of the reasons for the fall of that empire was the tremendous costs involved in policing and protecting any held lands, particularly India but also numerous other colonial holdings around the world. Thus, the economic stakes of imperialism cut both ways.

18. *"He was commonplace in complexion, in feature, in manner, and in voice"*: While reporting on the trial of the Nazi war criminal Adolf Eichmann, Hannah Arendt coined the phrase "the banality of evil," which posits that many of the greatest evils in the world originate in humans who are otherwise "normal" (that is, not sociopaths or madmen). This phrase also seems to apply to many imperialists in the Belgian Congo. Another interesting study of

something like this phenomenon is Christopher Browning's *Ordinary Men: Reserve Police Battalion 101 and the Final Solution in Poland*, which chronicles the lives of similarly "commonplace" men from Poland who were pressed into duty by the Nazis and essentially did as they were told, becoming proficient executioners in the process.

19. *"Otherwise there was only an indefinable, faint expression of his lips, something stealthy—a smile—not a smile—I remember it, but I can't explain. It was unconscious, this smile was, though just after he had said something it got intensified for an instant"*: In *The Great Gatsby* (1925), a novel that its author, F. Scott Fitzgerald, acknowledged was heavily influenced by *Heart of Darkness*, the narrator, Nick Carraway, describes Gatsby in intriguingly similar terms. In chapter 3, Nick relates:

> He smiled understandingly—much more than understandingly. It was one of those rare smiles with a quality of eternal reassurance in it, that you may come across four or five times in life. It faced—or seemed to face—the whole external world for an instant, and then concentrated on you with an irresistible prejudice in your favor. It understood you just so far as you wanted to be understood, believed in you as you would like to believe in yourself, and assured you that it had precisely the impression of you that, at your best, you hoped to convey. Precisely at that point it vanished—and I was looking at an elegant young rough-neck, a year or two over thirty, whose elaborate formality of speech just missed being absurd. Some time before he introduced himself I'd got a strong impression that he was picking his words with care.

20. *"When annoyed at meal-times by the constant quarrels of the white men about precedence, he ordered an immense round table to be made, for which a special house had to be built. This was the station's mess-room. Where he sat was the first place—the rest were nowhere. One felt this to be his unalterable conviction"*: The manager's unique interpretation of the famous round table that, in Arthurian legend, symbolized that all knights were of equal worth leads instead to each "knight" believing that his is the most important place at the table. It shows the manager to be cunning enough to be a leader at least of these men but driven by egotistical and selfish aims that are far from what the mythical Camelot would have endorsed. (For a more traditional rendering/explanation of the round table, see, among other films, *First Knight* [1995].)

21. *"the forest stood up spectrally"*: Early in the nineteenth century,

during what we now call the Romantic era (roughly 1790–1830), poets such as Wordsworth and Coleridge wrote often of a benevolent nature that could offer comfort, pleasure, and inspiration to humans. By the turn of the twentieth century, though, when *Heart of Darkness* appeared, literary movements like naturalism, along with evolving scientific developments, had combined to alter views of nature substantially, either displaying it as completely indifferent to humans or even in open opposition to humans' desires. In our own time, the view has evolved even further, with the environmental and green movements now suggesting that nature is *ours* to take care of and, in a sense, dependent upon *us* for its survival.

22. *"This simply because I had a notion it somehow would be of help to that Kurtz whom at the time I did not see—you understand. He was just a word for me. I did not see the man in the name any more than you do"*: This idea of believing without seeing has many important connections with literature and the movies. It is a central tenet of the Christian faith as expressed in the New Testament of the Bible. But we also find it in a number of films, perhaps most memorably (and startlingly) in the mysterious figure of Keyser Söze, portrayed by Kevin Spacey, in Bryan Singer's 1995 film *The Usual Suspects*. In the immediate context of the story, however, this "notion" has more to do with Marlow choosing the devil he *can't* see over the devils he *can*.

23. *"What more did I want? What I really wanted was rivets, by heaven! Rivets. To get on with the work—to stop the hole"*: Endlessly frustrated by the inefficiency he sees around him in the Congo, Marlow transfers his whole desire for order and efficiency onto the rivets that are so basic and plentiful in Europe and even at the previous station that he visited—and yet nearly impossible to find at this particular spot.

24. *"a rioting invasion of soundless life, a rolling wave of plants, piled up, crested, ready to topple over the creek, to sweep every little man of us out of his little existence"*: Conrad's language here echoes the fear of death at the hands of an all-powerful nature that is shared by the four men shipwrecked in Stephen Crane's short story "The Open Boat" (1897). Conrad and Crane became good friends late in Crane's all too brief life (he died in 1900 of tuberculosis at the age of only twenty-eight).

25. *"Instead of rivets there came an invasion, an infliction, a visitation"*: As countless historians have referenced, contact between "civilized" explorers and native peoples in lands throughout the world has often had fatal consequences for those peoples. This is because their immune systems have not had to fight off some of the germs carried by those from the outside world and are unable to adapt. This has

not always been true, though, as many young imperialists who accepted positions in Africa and other colonial lands died at the hands of diseases for which their own, fairly delicate immune systems were not prepared.

## PART II

1. *"'Ah! my boy, trust to this—I say, trust to this.' I saw him extend his short flipper of an arm for a gesture that took in the forest, the creek, the mud, the river"*: Unlike Marlow, who at least seems to reference Darwin correctly (see note 15 of Part I), the manager and his uncle rely on a slightly corrupted evolution of Darwinian concepts commonly known as social Darwinism, a belief that was particularly popular during late Victorian and early modernist times (roughly 1870 to World War I in the 1910s). Social Darwinism took the idea of "survival of the fittest" and tried to apply it among classes and even races of individuals both within and outside of "civilized" society. In the manager's case, his surprising longevity in the disease-ridden Congo creates in him what we might call a "Darwinian arrogance" that he will prove himself "fittest" simply by outliving all his rivals, including Kurtz. At the same time, Marlow mocks the idea that either the manager or his uncle (with his "short flipper of an arm") has any control over their survival, much less the mysterious and seemingly unknowable African jungle.

2. *"Fine fellows—cannibals—in their place. They were men one could work with, and I am grateful to them"*: The presence of "cannibals" in fiction had a long tradition well before Conrad wrote *Heart of Darkness*. The protagonists of Daniel Defoe's *Robinson Crusoe* (1719) and Herman Melville's *Typee* (1846), to name only two especially prominent examples, both live at least part of their exiled lives in fear of discovering cannibals.

3. *"we were travelling in the night of first ages, of those ages that are gone, leaving hardly a sign—and no memories"*: Developments in science and history moved so swiftly across the nineteenth century that the idea of the "primeval" for Victorians was a radically different one than ever before. Instead of a history of the world as brief as four thousand years based on some biblical accounts, the same history was considered to have covered countless millennia by the time Marlow described his travel in the "night of first ages." This lengthening of what we know as "history" continues, as the age of the universe increases virtually every time a more powerful deep space telescope is created.

4. *"you could see there a singleness of intention, an honest concern*

*for the right way of going to work, which made these humble pages, thought out so many years ago, luminous with another than a professional light"*: Marlow's fondness for the right kind of "work" ties his narrative to the mid-nineteenth-century works of Thomas Carlyle. This, along with some of his arguably racist and at least racially insensitive views, reminds us that *Heart of Darkness*, while often celebrated as a modernist text that points forward to the twentieth century, also is very much a product of the Victorian era that was ending just as it first appeared in 1899.

5. *"So, unless they swallowed the wire itself, or made loops of it to snare the fish with, I don't see what good their extravagant salary could be to them"*: Marlow's keen sense of cynicism and disgust for hypocrisy lead to a harsh indictment of how the crew is paid in "currency" that is literally worthless. A number of economic theorists before Conrad's time, including Adam Smith and Karl Marx, had considered the importance of what is known as the "use value" of a product. Given the right place and time, such wire might have such a value or even be prized as a commodity. But, in the isolation and danger of the Congo, such pay is less than worthless in Marlow's eyes.

6. *"Yes; I looked at them as you would on any human being, with a curiosity of their impulses, motives, capacities, weaknesses, when brought to the test of an inexorable physical necessity"*: Marlow's curiosity about others echoes Ishmael's fascination with his friend Queequeg and others from countries around the world in Herman Melville's *Moby-Dick*.

7. *"beset by as many dangers as though he had been an enchanted princess sleeping in a fabulous castle"*: In a surprising moment within such a dark tale, Marlow actually compares Kurtz to "an enchanted princess sleeping in a fabulous castle." His point here mainly is to emphasize the number of dangers that he has to face in order to rescue the highly valued person of Kurtz. But it also serves as a gentle reminder that he has not yet even *seen* Kurtz, who remains as artificial at this point as the princesses in fairy tales that we often tell to children.

8. *"Arrows, by Jove!"*: Marlow's slow-motion telling of the beginning of the attack, which Ian Watt famously described as "delayed decoding," replicates the confusion and ignorance that mark Marlow's initial response to the "sticks" he sees flying through the air. Though we might recognize these instantly for the arrows they are in one circumstance (say, if we saw video of such a battle), Conrad helps us to understand just how difficult it might be in the bewildering state of mind of Marlow to distinguish them during this astonishing and feverish attack.

9.  "*A deuce of a lot of smoke came up and drove slowly forward. I swore at it. Now I couldn't see the ripple or the snag either*": Though Marlow does not use the actual term, his words here point to a phenomenon known as the "fog of war." The term is usually credited to the Prussian military analyst Carl von Clausewitz, who wrote: "The great uncertainty of all data in War is a peculiar difficulty, because all action must, to a certain extent, be planned in a mere twilight, which in addition not infrequently—like the effect of a fog or moonshine—gives to things exaggerated dimensions and an unnatural appearance" (*On War*, book 2, chapter 2, paragraph 24).

10. "*The earth for us is a place to live in, where we must put up with sights, with sounds, with smells too, by Jove!—breathe dead hippo, so to speak, and not be contaminated*": Though it is delivered in language and imagery specific to his time in Africa, Marlow's declaration here points to the ongoing universality of Marlow's story and helps to explain why *Heart of Darkness*'s importance endures. Life is lived among diversity, including aspects that each individual dislikes, but life must be lived nevertheless, and each of us finds a way to adapt to our ever-changing world.

11. "*'By the simple exercise of our will we can exert a power for good practically unbounded,' etc., etc.*": This kind of language, promising that the West can and should "improve" places like Africa, was particularly prominent in some of the writings of Henry Morton Stanley (of Stanley and Livingstone fame) and King Leopold II of Belgium, who personally owned the Congo Free State (unlike most colonies, which were officially the possessions of nations, not persons). Though this belief often served only to hide less noble intentions (particularly the economic exploitation of colonies and their inhabitants), a longer view of history paints more of a mixed picture. Recent efforts by international organizations and a number of countries to fight diseases like AIDS and malaria have made at least some progress in a number of African nations within the last decade. At the same time, significant challenges and problems remain, some of which seem to require solutions either by individual African countries or by larger groups of African nations joining together in common effort (possibly including the current crisis in Darfur).

12. "*He won't be forgotten. Whatever he was, he was not common. He had the power to charm or frighten rudimentary souls into an aggravated witch-dance in his honour; he could also fill the small souls of the pilgrims with bitter misgivings*": This charismatic power to whip large crowds into a frenzy, to say and believe whatever is needed in order to take control of a village or country,

has unfortunately lived on in a number of real-life figures in modern African history, including Idi Amin Dada of Uganda in the 1970s (memorably portrayed by Forest Whitaker in the 2006 film *The Last King of Scotland*).

## PART III

1. *"'What can you expect?' he burst out; 'he came to them with thunder and lightning, you know—and they had never seen anything like it—and very terrible'"*: The harlequin tries to avoid speaking too directly here, but it is fairly clear that the phrase "thunder and lightning" refers to the guns that Kurtz has likely used in rampaging local villages. Using technology to achieve one's aims also lies at the heart of two novels that were written about a decade before *Heart of Darkness*. In Rudyard Kipling's *The Man Who Would Be King* (1888), two vagabonds briefly achieve power as kings over a fictional land near India by threatening the locals with guns (though they do, in true imperial fashion, eventually begin training their subjects how to use those same firearms as they form an army to protect them). In Mark Twain's *A Connecticut Yankee in King Arthur's Court* (1889), an American from the nineteenth century is transported into medieval times but gains respect by using modern ideas and technology (including knowledge of a solar eclipse) as "magic."

2. *"I could not hear a sound, but through my glasses I saw the thin arm extended commandingly, the lower jaw moving, the eyes of that apparition shining darkly far in its bony head that nodded with grotesque jerks"*: This statement is typical of the way that Marlow, telling after Kurtz's death of his encounter with the living Kurtz, still describes the enigmatic figure as a virtual skeleton or corpse. Perhaps in Marlow's mind, Kurtz was already dead, or at least destined to die, before Marlow reached him (which may have been the manager's plan all along (see note 1 of Part II).

3. *"'I anticipated this. Shows a complete want of judgment. It is my duty to point it out in the proper quarters'"*: Even deep in the Congo, office politics still exist. Living up (or actually down) to the petty reputation that Marlow has established for him, the manager insists on claiming just how right he was to doubt Kurtz and his "methods" in the first place. And such behavior leads Marlow to have even greater disgust for the manager, as his "I told you so" about Kurtz is almost more than he can stand.

4. *"My hour of favour was over. I found myself lumped along with*

*Kurtz as a partisan of methods for which the time was not ripe. I was unsound! Ah! but it was something to have at least a choice of nightmares"*: This is a complex and surprising moment in Marlow's narrative. Appalled by the naked hypocrisy of the Company men, especially the manager, Marlow embraces Kurtz and the violent methods that he has clearly employed to gain his bounty of ivory. But it is hard to imagine Marlow actually supporting the violence itself. Instead, he may simply accept Kurtz's behavior as brutal but honest instead of the hypocrisy and pretense of individuals like the manager and the brickmaker.

5. *"imagined myself living alone and unarmed in the woods to an advanced age"*: Marlow here imagines himself living the life of Robinson Crusoe in the midst of the African jungle rather than on a deserted isle. One of the most important works in the history of the novel, Defoe's *Robinson Crusoe* continues to inspire imitations to this day. In recent decades, Tim Severin's book *Seeking Robinson Crusoe* (2002) has renewed the search for Defoe's real-life model for Crusoe; J. M. Coetzee's *Foe* (1986) has fascinatingly retold the story from a woman's point of view; and Michel Tournier's *Friday* (1967) has offered Crusoe's story from the point of view of the titular character, who willingly serves as Crusoe's servant in Defoe's original tale. In addition, films including *Cast Away* (2000) have updated the famous story of Crusoe, while television recently offered *Lost* as well. The universe of artistic works generated by Defoe's enduring novel is well worth exploring, and growing larger all the time.

6. *"two thousand eyes followed the evolutions of the splashing, thumping, fiery river-demon beating the water with its terrible tail and breathing black smoke into the air"*: In a remarkable and unique moment in the narrative, Marlow describes the steamer as it would have appeared to the Africans rather than from his own perspective. Robert Louis Stevenson uses a similar technique with much greater regularity in his novella *The Beach of Falesá* (1893).

7. *"I saw on that ivory face the expression of sombre pride, of ruthless power, of craven terror—of an intense and hopeless despair"*: The idea of a person being transformed by an obsession with a particular object, as Kurtz's face comes to appear like "ivory" to Marlow, is also a key concept in another novel from the same period, Oscar Wilde's *The Picture of Dorian Gray* (1890). Wilde's novel, however, features a fascinating twist: as Dorian pursues his hedonistic ways, his physical appearance does not change—but a particular portrait of him grows ever uglier and more sinister as he continues to sin.

8. *"'Mistah Kurtz—he dead'"*: This succinct and brutal line (delivered "in a tone of scathing contempt") serves as one of two epigraphs to T. S. Eliot's poem "The Hollow Men" (1925). Eliot's title for this poem also serves as an appropriate term for many of the imperialists Marlow encounters—Marlow himself says of the brickmaker, "it seemed to me that if I tried I could poke my forefinger through him, and find nothing inside but a little loose dirt, maybe." Eliot's poem is also well known for its closing lines:

> This is the way the world ends
> This is the way the world ends
> This is the way the world ends
> Not with a bang but a whimper.

Also, note how these lines match up quite well with Marlow's ambivalent description of his struggle with death, which he calls "the most unexciting contest you can imagine."

9. *"the bearing of commonplace individuals going about their business in the assurance of perfect safety"*: This idea of members of society walking about in "the assurance of perfect safety" lies at the heart of Conrad's urban spy novel set in Victorian London, *The Secret Agent* (1907). Though quite different from some of Conrad's early efforts and focused instead on an English metropolis, *The Secret Agent* offers such a compelling vision of the mind-set behind terroristic behavior that it has received a great deal of attention in the wake of 9/11 and other attacks throughout the world.

10. *"I had some difficulty in restraining myself from laughing in their faces, so full of stupid importance. I daresay I was not very well at that time. I tottered about the streets—there were various affairs to settle—grinning bitterly at perfectly respectable persons"*: How Marlow feels upon his return to society again echoes Ishmael in his reasons for fleeing from society in the first place, as we see in the opening paragraph of Herman Melville's *Moby-Dick*: "Whenever I find myself growing grim about the mouth; whenever it is a damp, drizzly November in my soul; whenever I find myself involuntarily pausing before coffin warehouses, and bringing up the rear of every funeral I meet; and especially whenever my hypos get such an upper hand of me, that it requires a strong moral principle to prevent me from deliberately stepping into the street, and methodically knocking people's hats off—then, I account it high time to get to sea as soon as I can."

11. *"'He electrified large meetings. He had the faith—don't you see?—he had the faith. He could get himself to believe anything—*

*anything'"*: This type of rhetorical power can also be seen in a number of equally unforgettable figures in fiction and film, including 1930s Louisiana governor Huey Long and the character he inspired, Willie Stark, in Robert Penn Warren's *All the King's Men* (1946) (and in the Academy Award–winning 1949 film of the same name); Charles Foster Kane as portrayed by Orson Welles in the film *Citizen Kane* (1941); and Forest Whitaker's Idi Amin in *The Last King of Scotland* (2006).

12. *"She had a mature capacity for fidelity, for belief, for suffering"*: While critics tend to view Marlow's behavior in this scene as condescending toward the Intended and often women in general, it is interesting to note that the traits that Marlow attributes to her— fidelity, belief, suffering—were among those characteristics that Conrad often considered the most important, as he made clear in a number of letters during his career. In addition, Conrad noted in a 1902 letter to the magazine editor William Blackwood that he considered this scene important because it makes *Heart of Darkness* more than just the story of a white man in Africa.

13. *"her fair hair seemed to catch all the remaining light in a glimmer of gold"*: This reference to the Intended's "fair hair," coupled with Marlow's admission on the previous page that he cannot defend her from the "triumphant darkness," carries an odd hint of the fairy tale, similar to Marlow's earlier comparison of Kurtz to an "enchanted princess" similarly awaiting rescue (see note 7 of Part II).

# AVAILABLE FROM PENGUIN CLASSICS

*Chance: A Tale in Two Parts*

*Heart of Darkness*
Penguin Classics Deluxe Edition
Introduction by Adam Hochschild

*Lord Jim: A Tale*
Edited by J. H. Stape
Introduction by Allan Simmons

*The Nigger of the 'Narcissus'
and Other Stories*
Edited by Alan Simmons
Introduction by Gail Fraser

*Nostromo: A Tale of the Seaboard*
Edited with an Introduction
by Veronique Pauly

*The Portable Conrad*
Edited with an Introduction
by Michael Gorra

*The Secret Agent: A Simple Tale*
Edited by Michael Newton
with Senior Editor, J. H. Stape

*The Shadow-Line: A Confession*
Edited with an Introduction
by Jacques Berthoud

*Typhoon and Other Stories*
Edited with an Introduction
by J. H. Stape

*Under Western Eyes*
Edited with an Introduction
by Stephen Donovan

*Victory*
Edited by Robert Hampson with
an Introduction by John Gray

**PENGUIN
BOOKS**